LITERATURE AND THE CHANGING WORLD

Literature Breaking Barriers

BOOK NO. 8

Ivica Prtenjača
Let's Go Home, Son

managing editor
Sandra Ukalović

publisher
V.B.Z. d.o.o.
10010 Zagreb, Dračevička 12
tel: +385 (0)1 6235 419
fax: +385 (0)1 6235 418
e-mail: info@vbz.hr
www.vbz.hr

for co-publisher
Istros Books
Conway Hall, 25 Red Lion Square,
London, WC1R 4RL
e-mail: info@istrosbooks.com

for publisher
Mladen Zatezalo

editor
Susan Curtis

graphic editor
Siniša Kovačić

layout
V.B.Z. studio, Zagreb

cover design
Studio 2M, Zagreb

printed by
Denona d.o.o., Zagreb
August 2023

 Funded by the European Union. Views and opinions expressed are however those of the author(s) only and do not necessarily reflect those of the European Union or the European Education and Culture Executive Agency (EACEA). Neither the European Union nor EACEA can be held responsible for them.

Ivica Prtenjača
Let's Go Home, Son

Translated from the Croatian by
David Williams

v|b|z ZAGREB

2023

LITERATURE AND THE CHANGING WORLD

Literature Breaking Barriers

BOOK NO. 8

ORIGINAL TITLE
Ivica Prtenjača
Sine, idemo kući

Copyright © 2021 by Ivica Prtenjača and V.B.Z. d.o.o.
Translation © 2023 for UK edition David Williams
All rights reserved.

Copyright © 2023 for English edition:
V.B.Z. d.o.o., Zagreb
All rights reserved.

Republic of Croatia Ministry of Culture and Media Republika Hrvatska Ministarstvo kulture i medija

This book has been published with support from the Ministry of Culture and Media of the Republic of Croatia.

The product covered by the licence fulfils the ecological criteria for *"Graphic Paper"* (EU) 2019/70, valid from 11-01-2019 until 31-12-2024.

ISBN 978-1-912545-34-6

G O O N , tell me! What the hell did I do to you? Tell me!

Between two palm trees swaying in a furious northeaster, a young man stands outside the main entrance to the children's hospital, there near the shore itself. The rain turns to ice and bounces off his shoulders, his black coat already drenched in sleet from without and in sweat from within. The wind whips the salt from the dark churn of the water's surface, creating a hazy filter. It's the end of January, and God calls first with lightning, and then with a low-rumbling thunder.

Tell me! the man howls, his gaze fixed on the black squall of the sky.

Outside, it's early evening, which is also how it feels inside, in the hospital, where they're trying to save his son. The boy is nine days old. He won't stop crying, and when he can't cry anymore, he loses consciousness.

No one knows what's wrong with him.

I.

HE DRINKS lukewarm water from a half-empty bottle that he'll take with him in the ambulance. He'll keep it on the pillow, on the narrow stretcher in the back. Outside, it's spring. In the ambulance, it could be any season at all.

He has to go to hospital for observation. He's frail, and for most of the day he breathes through a tube in his nose, dragging it behind him like a tail, barely able to shuffle around the house. At mealtimes, she takes the tube out and switches off the oxygen concentrator (to give its motor a rest), and it's only then that quiet returns, the normal inhalation and exhalation of breath, the banging of cutlery, the simmering of food in the pot. Flames crackle in a woodstove, its crooked flue almost warping a room both modest and uncluttered. The skeletal kitchen his parents got as part of the reconstruction effort, for homes damaged or destroyed in the war, is already showing signs of age. There's a Catholic calendar stuck to the door, and a row of those stickers the priest gives you when he blesses the house. In a thin gold frame on the wall there's a watercolour of a fish, a few photos of their grandson carefully sellotaped beside it. Above the table and its four chairs hangs the cheapest Ikea clock. That was from me. Next to the kitchen is the living room, then a narrow hallway that leads to the bathroom and down towards the larder with its two tall stainless barrels, one for wine, the other for oil. In the living room, a three-seater couch and a cabinetta (his word) with glasses and a dinner set, its drawers home to two broken pressure gauges, another one that works, and the resuscitators that the sickness outgrew. Next to the Quadro television, whose remote never worked properly, there's a little meter that measures the oxygen in blood, laid out on a paper towel where everyone can see it.

 This morning, when the transfer ambulance pulled up outside, the driver and the very young nurse were running an hour late, because they're always late when they have to take someone to Zagreb. Mum and Dad have been ready since four o'clock. They've got a carry bag with essentials: a bottle of water, biscuits wrapped in a serviette in a plastic bag, cash, and a yellow envelope stuffed with test results going back years; the natural history of an illness. At the hospital, no one's ever looked at them, but she's always hoped that they'd find a new treatment buried in there. Then the pills, so many pills. She's never sure whether they'll have what he needs, so she brings them all, just in case, gives them to the nurse, or, if she's lucky, the doctor. They can't just leave him there, she tells me, while we wait for him to be admitted and transferred to his room on the third floor.

It'd been a difficult trip and his back had hurt. She'd tried to apply a kind of cream, but couldn't manage it, both of them holding tight to his cot so they didn't fall over. The ambulance had lurched from side to side as the driver accelerated, chatting idly to the nurse, who had joined him up front. 'So I don't get in your way,' that's what she'd said. In a pudgy little paw with garishly manicured nails, she'd cradled a mobile phone, the stream of messages endless, her eyes lighting up every time it pinged. 'No worries at all, you just go,' my mother had nodded to the girl of twenty. She'd barely looked at my father, who was swaddled in a blanket and on oxygen.

I met them in the tiny parking area. The nurse went inside to fetch a wheelchair to bring him inside. 'It's what we're here for, isn't it,' she'd said, still cradling her pet Huawei. He was exhausted, and we hugged. Mum gave me a kiss. It's not the first time I've met them here, not his first rodeo. We know the drill, the whole ecosystem, the air freighted with fear and helplessness. There's a queue at admissions. He sits there in his wheelchair, asks for water. Drinks.

'I can't breathe properly,' he says.

That's him for you, a man almost apologetic that he can't get enough air, a man who doesn't want to create a fuss, doesn't want to disturb anyone, or, worse still, draw attention to himself. We've been waiting half an hour and they haven't even given us a bottle of oxygen. I bend down to the gap in the glass so I don't have to raise my voice, but the woman inside pre-empts me, insists that I wait, that I not come any closer, and that everything will be fine. I'm not sure how she hit upon that exact order, whether it was by syllogism or just experience. And I don't know how she knew what I wanted to say, or why it was such a problem for me to tell her that we needed a bottle of oxygen, because the man's lungs don't work and his face has gone grey. Because he's suffocating.

...Excuse me, I know what I'm trying to tell you is pretty awkward, this being a hospital for folk with lung problems and all, it's really not the time or place, but if you could perhaps send someone to fetch us just that one bottle, I mean surely, even here on the ground floor, dire as it is, you'd have to have a few untouched bottles of that lifesaving oxygen. And yes, I know I'm getting a bit lippy, but would you kindly shelve your important protocols and let me get my head down near that magical aperture, just for a second, so that I can quietly tell you what's what. Scout's honour, when we get that bottle, that's it, I won't ask for anything else, I won't ask any more questions, you won't see or hear from me again...

A tall, thin paramedic in a green coat headed our way, his white pants way too short.

'Let's roll, Captain,' he says, scooting behind the wheelchair.

'But he doesn't have a bottle,' my mother almost wails.

'We're going straight up, straight to his room, don't you worry,' the paramedic replies.

We stood aside as he wheeled Dad to the lift. In the blink of an eye, Mum, Dad, and the hospital's clone of a rangy dark-haired angel took off for heaven, to the clear plastic tube hanging from the wall above the bed in room number six. I hoofed it up the stairs, the lift too cramped for the son to go along for the ride. In the room, the angel helped Dad sit down on the bed, still in his jacket and fully dressed, before lying him down and putting a tube in his nose.

'Just a little for now. We'll get you changed when you're feeling better,' said the mouth on the tanned face, the hands and feet having already left the room. To fetch a new patient, for a new journey.

Someone was taking photos, but only years later will I remember who it was with the big shiny Pentax around his neck, its thin leather strap under his wide white collar, the figure slipping through the crowd, clicking away, then sliding the film in the back pocket of his blue flares. He was a distant relative, Josip, who people called Jole, and he was back in the village of his birth for the first time since he'd fled Yugoslavia at seventeen, first to Italy, then to Toronto, back to see the mama who'd nursed him with her milk, and the papa who'd nourished him with stories of Croatia, back for the wedding of his elder brother's daughter. At Frankfurt Airport, he'd rented a gold Audi 100, got behind the wheel, and without stopping (except for petrol and a piss, or so he told us), sped to the motherland he'd previously fled because he hadn't wanted to serve a criminal army. And, it has to be said, because he hadn't had much else to hang around for, just the general disarray of a semiliterate hick future in which hot blood coursed in a body too tight.

By the seventh grade, that future didn't interest him much, so he took up hunting. He shot rabbits, partridges, whatever, and hardly ever missed. When there was nothing to hunt, he'd plug a few into a tree, a road sign, or a stray dog. 'It's not a car, it's a rocket ship,' - that's what he told folk when they'd stare at the limousine in which he'd arrived. Although he had a Canadian passport, he hadn't quite lost his fear of state security or the police. But it was nothing he couldn't manage. Tito had been dead a couple of years: 'Had'da wait for the pig to rot, didn't wanna come before, but I coulda, I ain't scared.' For all the swagger, he was a dead man walking, torn somewhere between a life lived in a far-off land and memories of his boyhood days here in the village. He figured that if he really rocketed, only stopping for petrol and a piss, he'd make it back to the time before he left. He wanted that quarter of a century to vanish in the air, like an illusion, desperately hoping that his kin would be there to welcome him home, where, with his Ray Bans, his flash wheels, and his hard currency, he'd enter among them like a king. And here he was, Joe the Builder, construction worker in the suburbs of Toronto, ready to grab his shotgun and put both barrels into something with a pulse, something warm and full of blood. But that world had gone, and for a month that stretched on forever, Jole tiptoed around, clicking away, slipping the films in his back pocket and storing them in a shoe box under the sofa bed, the same one from which he'd set off into the world. He slept in the old part of the house, in a room with no windows, just shutters and three iron bars to stop anyone from stealing in and making off with the poverty that filled the house to perfection.

At his niece's wedding, he's just the same. In a shirt with lace and gold trim on the collar, he's up on the terrace, zooming in on the scene a few metres below. Beside a white car, the Croatian tricolour tied in a bow to its chrome rear view mirror, and the same tricolour, only wider, stretched across the bonnet, stands a man in a dark tie and a blue short-sleeved shirt, brown sunglasses with fake gold frames on his face, a Seiko watch on his wrist. He's leaning on the fender of a Fiat 1300, smiling straight at the camera, a group of children playing nearby. There's a woman with her back turned, pinning a sprig of rosemary to the pocket of a guy with a bushy moustache and a red and black cap, the rosemary braided with a tricolour ribbon. Her hand's blurry, which means she's moving. Beside the fence, there's a car parked under a big mulberry tree which is yet to offer any shade, the sun still in the east. It's not even noon, the globe hasn't turned, clocks haven't chimed midday. The world is standing still, the way it always does in moments of little and great consequence.

The hand that took the shot was the hand of a killer. Might this explain why the photo is so full of life? And is the contradiction an attempt at redemption, or a show of remorse? Or did chance arrange things this way? If so, chance did its work well. I love this photo.

What makes this arbitrary moment, this summer snapshot from a village wedding, so special? It's because there in his tie, sunglasses, and watch, next to his shiny car, he's smiling. He, a man more accustomed to clogs, a short white dust-coat, and thick white cotton pants, the uniform in which he glides around the bakery, a sack of yeast in hand, about to mix it with eighty litres of water and a mountain of flour. A man more accustomed to the heavy canvas trousers and ragged shirt in which he'd swing a sledgehammer at a steel peg gripped in the hand of a terrified, dark-haired woman, my mother. They're punching holes in the blue stone, holes where they'll stick dynamite to level a section of the steep slope for their house: for the foundations of a quiet life. One in which dynamite explodes and a sledgehammer glistens in the heat of the afternoon, before a quick wash-up and hectic dash to the bakery. He was often worried and weary, and he seldom smiled, but when he did, he did so with such emotion, as if someone had just blessed him with sunken treasure, the riches of the world. He's smiling now, almost posing, his clear blue eyes looking straight at the dark face of the Pentax. Is he posing? When I'd look at the photo as a boy, and then later as a young man, I was ashamed of the thought. Of the posing, of the possibility of it. No way, he'd never do that, not ever, not even now, not even when machines from a hospital basement are pumping air up into his lungs. He didn't fake it, didn't pretend.

But here, in this *mise-en-scène*, in this fragment of life curated by Jole's careless hand and lazy eye, he's in a film poster, leaning against a car of glimmering chrome, his eyes hidden behind brown-tinted lenses, kids frozen at play beside him. The tricolour is stretched across the white sheet metal of the hood, the car's side mirror reflecting a vague shadow. What's this film about? And who on earth is this man? He's not my father, no way. He's not the apprentice baker, the playground rebel who the teacher caned in front of the class for vanishing into the corn fields with a friend when they were supposed to be out picking cherries. Passing the time, the classmate, who may or may not have led Dad astray, discovered that you could make little balls from the damp soil, and then with a small rock and some twigs, that you could knock together a man, a family, a village, an entire world. When they got back to school, the cane didn't touch his friend. But my father, he got twenty strokes on his open palm. He never forgave the teacher, nor the school, the village, the state, or even the world. Beating a kid for fuck's sake. That's what he used to say. That's what we grew up with.

That kid isn't in the film poster. Somewhere along the way, that hurt little boy, who grew up in defiant poverty and an absence of love, had managed to shed his skin. When he'd raise the sledgehammer, Mum would take a deep breath and wind every muscle tight, but she'd never let that steel wedge go. She'd clasp it the way desperate people cling to shadows, to glimmers of hope in the future. When he'd strike, her compressed lungs would release a scream piercing everything in sight. And so it went for hours: the strike, the scream, the silence. Until the blue stone's dark twisted veins were completely ruptured. Tomorrow she'll insert the dynamite, her nimble fingers threading the wick under the heavy steel net he'd laid out. Then she'll head back to the hut, get me up out of my cradle, wrap my head in a blanket and put her hands over my ears. And then he'll light the wick and roar *dynamite*! Seconds later the dynamite will explode, pulverising the stone, the baker's operation planned to perfection. The man I'm looking at in the photo isn't the guy doing the dynamiting. This guy's almost a playboy. But not really. He isn't showing off, isn't trying to seduce anyone. He's just leaning there on his car, at a village wedding about to get underway, looking up at that dipshit Jole who's yanked his blue trousers so far up that his whole sack is wedged over to the right, a bulging anatomical relief among the old boys still in their traditional lined pants. A pair of cobalt blue balls standing there on the terrace, photographing the wedding. What had Jole been waiting for all those years, I wonder, why didn't he come back sooner? Here in the backwoods, he's as beautiful as a mistake.

Why is the man smiling? What's happening up there on the terrace? I try to remember, because I'm one of the kids beside the car. Back turned, my hair as thick as a helmet, the tight contour of my shirt betraying my love of food. I'm holding something in my hand. A glass, half full.

I remember the seconds before my father leaned on the bonnet, and I remember something of the time after, but the actual moment he smiled and held his gaze to the camera, I don't. A stray dog, skinny and half-lame, with legs that would have been white if they weren't matted with dirt, was chasing a tall, brown horse, a chain trailing from its neck, its flanks drenched in great swathes of sweat. As it galloped past the wedding guests and their cars, the bride let out a scream, and her mother grabbed a piece of firewood and threw it at the horse. The piece of wood flew straight across the road, landing with a thud against a stone wall, centimetres from the head of a little girl who was picking lollies from the dust. The dog was yelping for its life, as if hunting a rabbit or a fox, while the horse, spurred more by the sudden freedom to stretch its legs than any fear of the pursuing mutt, bolted on, shoes clacking on the smooth cobbled path where we stood as still as statues.

'Faark me, that's Pilip's nag!'

Someone recognised the animal, which having pulled up a few metres away, was now staring at us, its flared nostrils pumping out enormous rings of steam. Raising its head, it looked exactly like the horse on the hundred dinar note, one of which, coincidentally, I had in my pocket. Grandad had given it to me in case I needed to buy something at the wedding. Neither he nor I had any idea why I might need money in a village that didn't have a shop, particularly when I was at our distant relative's wedding, surrounded by everything I could ever want, fly-kissed and gratis. Now even the dog had stopped, and was panting away. An old woman clocked it with a stick and it scampered. The horse then lowered its head, what was left of its chain lying on the cobbled path. In his flat-soled shiny shoes, the postman, a total runt, ran over and jumped on the chain, thinking that he'd restrain the horse. That was the plan. Someone had to get hold of the horse and get it out of there, so that this static and monotonous film could continue, with its singing and yelling, and eating and drinking, the volleys of laughter and non-stop swearing, which is how people communicated their overwhelming sense of life's fullness, and their fatal lack of other words to express happiness, rapture, surprise, or just their best wishes ('alltha best t'the bride 'n groom, alltha fuckin' best!'). All of this needed to ooze and run like the sap from a fig tree, down along the grizzled crust of life and into the earth itself. Because when that first drop sinks into the dirt, this life will cease. But until that happens, let no one interrupt this chaotic and surreal summer day as it turns towards the sun. Let life take its course, and let these two young folk, who just yesterday were still kids, let them slip away into their future and, at least for a moment, hope for something there. Hope seemed important to me when I was a child, really got me excited. I knocked back my glass of wine and went for a refill.

'I'll fucking get you now,' the postman bawled, stamping on the thick chain. But when the horse suddenly yanked its neck up, his weedy legs and shiny shoes skidded across the butter-smooth stone. Like something out of Stan Lee, Mile, our postman, flew high in the air and landed on his back, his head thumping on the ground. The horse galloped off down the street, the white dog, hidden by the fence, in hot pursuit.

People hurried over to where Mile lay flat on his back, out cold. A woman poured half a bottle of slivovitz into a cloth and started rubbing it on his face, but Mile couldn't be roused. She kept at it, and before long he had slivovitz running down his cheeks, like tears. Eyes still shut, our postman contorted his mouth and hunted down those little rivulets, taking the medicine he'd taken so many times before. 'No blood, not a fucking scratch on me,' he said, springing to his feet.

Had the comedy of it all kept the smile on my father's face? He loved simpletons, contrarians, folks with loose screws, the impious and obstinate, those who swore for the hell of it. Even more so, he loved people who could spin a yarn about these kinds of characters. But he couldn't handle being among them. They were tiresome, difficult, capricious, couldn't hold it together. They irritated him, so he steered well clear. He was always serious, wary somehow, always on guard. He was a workhorse and an autodidact. He taught himself how to build a house, use explosives, lay concrete. The only instruction he ever got was at the vocational high school where he'd trained to become a baker, taught by an old bag who owned both the bakery and the house where he lived with two of his classmates. In what passed as work experience, he'd unloaded sacks of flour, fed and mucked out the animals that the landlord and his wife kept in stables out the back of the house, on the edge of town.

I remember Dad trying to plaster the ceiling of our bungalow. He mixed some runny concrete and tossed it in the air with a trowel, hoping it would stick. He stood on an upturned tin drum, while I filled the concrete bucket down below. I was twelve years old, and I remember that winter morning because before we settled into our work, I'd watched Kubrick's *A Space Odyssey* for the first time, wonder-struck, and in near ecstasy at what I'd seen and barely understood. Dad couldn't get the hang of the hand movement, the secret angle you needed to toss the runny mix in the air, spread it out, and have it stick to the ceiling. He tossed it up vertically. And vertically it fell back down on his head, getting in his eyes. Not wanting to hide, I remained at my father's side, sharing his torment, so it fell on me too. He tossed two full buckets up, and when it all fell down, I'd faithfully pick it up, add a bit of water, and dump the lot back in the bucket. He eventually got down, lit a cigarette, and parked himself up on a concrete block, staring at his watch. He had to go to work soon. Night-shift at the bakery. He sat in silence, resolute and undefeated, yet somehow angry. He took a few more drags, jumped back up on the drum, scooped up half a trowel's worth and tossed it up at the ceiling, first one, then another, then another. It had started to stick. He'd figured out the movement. His face was covered in splashes of concrete, his right eye bloody from the lime. I wanted to say something, relieve him of the anger, cheer him up. But he just kept at it, only stopping to smooth the plaster out before cranking back into it. When we finally finished and we'd used up the whole mix, he hopped down and looked at me.

'We knocked the bastard off, aye.' And it was only then that I could breathe out, let my chest swell with joy and the sense of accomplishment, as if I'd shaken the burden of that crushing unrendered ceiling.

That's how I felt even now. I finished my wine, a whole glass of red with a few ice cubes that Dajana, the bride's youngest sister, had brought me from the house. 'Tastes like crap when it's warm,' she'd said. And true enough, it went down a treat with the ice.

He wasn't smiling because of the postman.

Was he smiling at me, at my wine? Had he even noticed that I was drinking? He wouldn't have stopped me, everyone drinks here, particularly at weddings. Things just get put in front of you. Come to think of it, people were more worried about the old folk than the kids. That morning, when we were behind the house helping turn the spit lamb, the two old blokes who were supposed to be in charge got so drunk that us kids had to finish the job. We stoked the fire, smeared the fat, made sure everything didn't end up in the ashes. We even turned the heavy wooden stakes with the five impaled lambs. Boris ran inside and came back with a loaf of bread, which we tore into chunks and rubbed over the lamb, soaking up the fat and juices. Then we sprinkled the bread with salt and scoffed it down. We swigged a bit of wine too, but not too much. But we were still starving, and before I knew it, I'd hacked a hunk of meat off a hind leg with a little knife. We quickly divvied it up and wolfed that down too. It was sacrilege. You don't touch a lamb on the spit until it's fully done, until it's had time to rest and you've carved it. But our high priests were plastered, dozing lazily in the shade of a mulberry tree, like saints. We threw a few potatoes in the embers, covering them with ash, for later. But we forgot all about them when the young guys came to bring the roast lamb inside. We trailed behind them in their white shirts and gelled hair, their taut bodies jacked with testosterone, happy and strong and reckless.

'Won't be too long before we'll be taking the roast in,' said Boris, with delight.

Two doctors and a nurse exited the lift, jolting me awake in my plastic chair. Stacked beside me were parts for the new lift they're going to build in the boarded-up hole. How they found a cavity like that in the building, I don't know, but next time we come, we'll take a spacious new lift to the third floor. Maybe the hospital staff will keep using this small old one.

How else to explain their good humour as they make their rounds of the critically ill. All the way to the glass doors, where you either need a swipe card or someone to buzz you in, the three of them look like they're about to burst out laughing.

Isn't that both scandalous and somehow glorious at the same time? I can live with the ambiguity. When they entered, and the door was slightly ajar, I could see Dad sitting up in bed, Mum feeding him, removing the oxygen mask before each mouthful. It was only then that I could see the tiredness in his eyes. I'd hoped to catch a little anger in there too, the abiding rage that had plastered the ceiling. But I could only detect the exhaustion, made worse by each mouthful of food. I waved, just a few metres away, having caught the door with my foot when the three of them went in. Mum motioned for me to join her. He had a double room to himself, the television on the wall showing the fairy tale of Dubrovnik's city walls. 'Sit down,' he says, 'get a chair.' I can barely understand him through the mask, but I'm relieved that he's conscious.

'Are you going to come this afternoon?' he asks.

'You know we are,' Mum replies.

'Ask the doctor when I can go home,' he says.

'I will, but you'll be here three or four days at least, so they can do the tests and stuff. You can't get that medicine any other way. You have stay here under observation for a few days and then only a panel can prescribe it,' I explain.

'I know all that, but ask them anyway, maybe they'll tell you.'

That's a man clinging to a thin thread of hope, to something that long ago plunged down into that ugly crater for the new lift, vanishing into the earth together with its secrets. That's the reality of the third floor. Mum flicked the channel, 'there's nothing to watch anyway,' she explained. There really isn't. An old clip of a crooner doing *Window to the Sunset*. It's a bracing spring morning in Zagreb. The nurse from the lift enters the room, addresses my father by his first name, remembering him from the last time he was here. He smiles.

I forgave her everything. It's that kind of place.

All of a sudden, the world smacks me in the face like that runny plaster. Cloudy, like something dissolved in the bottom of a glass, a gummy fluid is running down my face in heaving torrents, soaking into my limbs, gluing the tendons together, fusing my bones, the liquid metal streaming into my joints and hardening. Pewter. I remember it. There are a few rods in the sideboard drawer, but I can't reach them. I know they're there though, because my grandad uses them to patch the still. We'd melt it together, dripping it in the cracks. The shiny drops would quickly harden, and now they've bound my hands and legs and frozen me here to the spot. But the world keeps spinning, and the plaster through which I'm trying to look won't stop running down my face, down my forehead and the length of my mouth. I've lost the battle to remain upright. A tantrum won't help, even if I could muster one. I don't dare curse, because that would just make it more embarrassing. I can't move a muscle, and yet the world just keeps spinning around and around. Splayed out on the sofa bed, at times I feel like I'm flying, the way rotten leaves fly around your feet, a momentary, inglorious flapping. Through the gaps in the shutters, I can see people moving about in the yard, a few guys horsing around, singing, slurring words in each other's faces, their eyes narrow, their cheeks rosy.

They're drunk. And so am I.

For the first time in my life, I'm flat on my back wondering whether I'm going to survive. Out of nowhere, a wave of pleasure rushes over me, and not knowing any better, I chalk it up to the excitement of the wedding, to this bucolic summer revelry. To my parents, in their plain, city clothes, so different to all the country bumpkins cutting loose in their white shirts and folksy outfits, not to mention those who work abroad and their fancy get-up. My straitlaced parents don't sing, don't make a spectacle of themselves, they just smile. It'll pass, I tell myself, waiting for the nausea. I can't move, and that being the case, I'm probably going to spew all over myself. But the nausea never arrives, and I almost start to enjoy my helplessness. If this is it, if there's no pain, I'm probably not going to die either.

Do I dare fall asleep? My heart was pounding, and when I shut my eyes, the sound was ominous, every beat a temptation too great for my solitude. Fear was slithering its way through this liquid world, and it wasn't long until I opened my mouth and started howling, calling out for my father. He was only a few metres away, on the other side of the window, leaning on his car, smiling. But he didn't hear me. At first, my vocal cords were inhibited by shame, but I soon let out a guttural and mighty cry.

'Dad! Dad, help! Help!'

'Leave him, let him rest for a bit,' says my mother as I jiggle his hand, his eyes remaining shut. The oxygen machine drones away, his ribcage rising only ever so slightly. I stroke his forehead, gathering up a handful of the world, before quickly covering my palm with my other hand, so the world doesn't disappear.

I'd caught half a second of immortality.

Soon the cars roared into life and people started honking their horns, forming a procession that would make its way through the village, first to the registry office, then to the church, which was surrounded by cypress trees, and then finally, to the recited promises of eternal love, before God and man. How is it that sometimes everything goes bad, I asked myself, totally sloshed. How is it that women become ugly from one day to the next, and that men die of heart attacks while draining the dregs of a bottomless glass. Or they drop dead at work, having secretly downed one of those tiny bottles, which apparently they call grandkiddies. I almost slap myself on the forehead at how lucky I am. My grandad wouldn't dream of doing something like that, and neither would my father. None of us would.

We're not alkies. Not a single one of us. We're not unhappy. Are we?

I'm almost raving. Outside, someone had leaned himself up against the shutters, his bulging back pressing into the brown slats, a wretched sight if there ever was. It was as if someone had cut something rotten into the innocence of today's celebration, carved the lattice of future ruin into the purity of the very vow towards which the drunken procession will soon make its way, flags and accordion in tow. But what could really end in ruin? That's what I wondered as the broad fleshy back pressed itself into the timber slats. A marriage can't fall apart, that's not how things work here. No one in the village has ever divorced, it's impossible. Which means that everything will be fine, or, more to the point, that what will be will be. They'll bring children into the world, slip the axe of ruin in their hands, and as these children grow, first they'll blunt it, then they'll smelt it, and then when they're old enough, they'll forge a new one, bigger, heavier, and sharper, and with it, all over again, they'll shatter any kind of love or happiness, just enough to keep the circle of life turning, like a ring dance on a sinking road.

Let the wheel turn, let it all come tumbling down.

The white shirt moved off away from the shutters, but before doing so, a hand coming out of it hurled an empty bottle at a big blue steel door, the glass shattering everywhere, showering an old baba sitting on a rock in the yard. She'd just taken off her headscarf, intending to retie it. Her hair was now full of little shards of green glass which I could see glistening in the sun. She didn't say anything, just gently shook her hair, retied her kerchief, and sat perched there next to her walking stick. Outside, they can't get themselves organised, can't get moving. I can hear swear words and a song being butchered. Where do the bride and groom go, and what about the witnesses, the parents, the guests, does anyone know how these things are done?

'We're not fucking gypsies, folks, wait, now we've got it, careful...'

They headed off, and I was left alone with the old baba in the remnants of her glass crown. Suddenly, she disappeared too, having moved out of the sun that was now streaming through the mulberry tree. I'm not scared of dying any more, I can lift my head, can even move my hands. I'm going to get up, try and make it to the bathroom. I'll lie down in the bath, run the cold water. See what happens. I stared down at the tips of my too-big shoes, which I'd borrowed from a neighbour. My eyes travelled down along the two sharp ironed creases of my linen trousers. Although the creases were still straight, my eyes kept dropping, and it took a superhuman effort to lift them back up. I'd squint one eye and aim for my shoes, and I'd almost be there, but then it'd slump back down to my ankle. Even though the nausea was on the march, fermenting inside me, I figured that it wasn't yet time to get up. At some point, it was going to look for an exit, to come out into this festive afternoon, which had finally fallen silent. I can't do it on the bed, no way. I rolled over onto my side and let myself topple down onto the wooden floor. From there, I'd crawl, haul myself into the bathroom and lock the door. Maybe lean up against the washing machine, at least try to remain upright.

Here I go now. I toppled off the bed, landing on my right shoulder and face, not managing to get my hand down in time. The lower half of my body collapsed behind me like a corpse. It hurt, but it also woke me up. Winded by the fall, I needed a rest before I could start my crawl. I rolled over onto my stomach, lifted myself up on my elbows and tried to wriggle forward. The floorboards were rough-sawn and unvarnished, and my legs were dead weight, no help at all. I'd barely moved a few centimetres. I'm not going to make it, no chance. Why didn't Dad come, couldn't he hear me? Was I even yelling? Had my voice penetrated this fading afternoon, its blue-tinged images now furiously swirling and coalescing? What was I going to do?

The door opened and I saw two feet in black woollen socks, strapped up in sandals, then a white peasant blouse and a craggy face with a scarf tied firmly under the chin. The old girl.

'You sleeping, boyo?' she enquired.

'I'm sleeping, baba,' I replied, thinking ahead. I desperately wanted her to go before she twigged. And besides, she's too skinny to be of any help.

'Want something to drink? You thirsty, hungry?'

'No thanks, baba. I'm okay.'

She shuffled out and closed the door. Groaning, I gave a heave and again started to wriggle forward, but it was as if the ground kept sliding away from me, and for a second it felt like I was crawling up a steep ascent, up a winding mountain path, through the clouds.

I sat up against the door, leaned back, grabbed the handle, and flopped out into the hallway. It'll be better going here, with the floor tiles, just a little further and I'd be saved. And that's what happened. The creases on my trousers were like skates, and I almost glided my way to the bathroom. I managed to close the door, slither into the bath, find the tap, and turn the water on. First to float were my ginormous black shoes, a pair of moccasins with *vero cuoio* on the part where the sole doesn't touch the ground. Now they were floating like a pair of gondolas. Wonderful indeed, I thought to myself, before leaning my head over the side of the bath and throwing up on the floor. I grabbed the showerhead and hosed the mess towards the drain in the middle of the room. The red wine lost its colour and disappeared down the hole. I sprayed water all over the bathroom, even on the walls, and when I'd finished washing up, I breathed a sigh of relief. Then I spotted a small electric heater next to the washing machine, so I sprayed that too.

I saw the flaming current race up through the stream of water, down the showerhead, and then over my hand, splitting my heart into two crooked halves. I'm dead, killed by an electric shock, in a bath half-full of water, a pair of shoes bobbing gently on the surface. But then I noticed that the plug wasn't in the power socket. And so life returned, as it must, with a new problem. I'd drenched the socket, meaning that the first person to turn the power on was going to get electrocuted, and I, as they say, would have that engraved on my soul. As wasted and tragic as I was, I didn't want that. For a start, I'm carrying enough shit around already. But speaking of the soul, how can I have something engraved on it when I don't even know where it is, when I don't even believe that it exists. When I finally pull myself together, I'm going to take that bloody heater out to the rubbish pile and bury it in all the other crap. But until then, I'm just going to hold my head here in the cold water, among the gondolas.

'Darling, are you hungry?' my mother asks.

He waves a no. Tries to take the oxygen mask off and say something, but he can't, because tonight they've tied his hands to the bed. It's normal for patients like him, otherwise they rip the mask off and then their oxygen falls. 'It's better this way, safer,' the nurse explained when I called her over to untie him.

'How did you sleep, Dad?'
'I didn't.'

Instead of waking me up, the water makes me sleepy. My head has slumped over, and if someone hadn't tried the handle on the other side of the door and one of the gondolas hadn't bumped me on the forehead, I'd have sunk into an underwater dreamworld, which would've looked pretty freaky. I've locked the bathroom door, which means no one can reach me here. But someone's calling my name. It's a girl's voice and I know who. It's Vivien. She's crossed the frozen tundra, straight from Ken Parker's grave where she's laid flowers for the last time. He lies there in the icy earth, his insides ruptured, bear claws buried in his pelvis. There's also a bullet in his heart. He'd managed to cut short the agony when a bear got him one freezing winter dawn. It should've been sleeping, but there you go, obviously it wasn't. It was killing.

'In here, Vivien, Vivien, in here, save me!'

But the door was locked.

I dragged myself up and stood in the bath. I'm not going to die, that much is clear. I'm going to be fine. But how can I move my feet and stay upright when everything is so slippery and you're not there behind the door anymore, Vivien? I can't hear your voice. Who'll save me now, protect me, put that terrifying bear to sleep when it suddenly wakes up and comes after me as I wander this barren and frozen land. Vivien. Uuuuuu, I sang for a moment. Boozing is beautiful, liberating somehow. But it's also terrifying, because you see death in everything. I shuddered at the thought of the heater.

With my head pounding, I cradle my forehead and slowly return to the land of the living. I'm now going to put one foot in front of the other, and go sit on the toilet seat, dry off a bit. First I chucked my shoes out, and then, holding on to the vent that jutted out from the wall, I stepped into the middle of the bathroom. It was a good feeling, to stand, to see my reflection in the mirror, to be able to hold my head up. I bent over to let the water out of the bath. And threw up again. I'll be fine now, onwards and upwards. I sat down on the closed the lid of toilet seat and decided to take a short nap.

Outside, someone fired a shotgun. I heard two explosions, followed by the snap of the barrel, the reloading, and two more monstrous booms. The bathroom only has a small high window and I'd have to climb up on the bath to see what's going on. And I can't manage that. Who's shooting, and why? And then I remembered that the wedding guests must be coming back from the church about now, which means that this must be the welcoming party. I'm certain that it's Jole, always wanting to be part of the action. It could've been a hunter, but it's not, it's the nervy photographer, the flamboyantly dressed emigrant with a theory about everything. His favourite being the one about how in Canada, garbos get the most money. The state pays them extra because they think the stink's a health risk. Someone once asked him why he was a builder and not a garbo. 'Why, doesn't fucking matter why,' Jole shrugged, a sly expression on his face. 'That's how things turned out. I do what I fucking do.'

'Did you ask when I can go home?'

'The day after tomorrow. But it depends on the test results,' I reply.

'What tests did they do today, do you know?' Mum asks.

'The usual. Bloods, blood pressure, spirometry. They measured the gasses. The doctor says things aren't good.'

'Don't worry, it'll be fine. Did they tell you why you're back on 15 litres of oxygen when it was 12 yesterday?' I ask.

He shrugs his shoulders.

'Flour,' he whispers.

'What kind of flour, darling?' Mum asks, the fear bubbling in her eyes.

'The doctor says it's all because of the flour. That when it gets into your lungs, you get sick.'

The yard was soon full of song and clamour. A few cars are still parking on the roadside, honking their horns, everything getting perilously closer to me and my hideout. It's only a matter of time until someone comes knocking. The tables where people are going to sit are set up in the neighbour's yard, on the other side of a dead-end country road, but the gates are open, and people are milling about, and it wouldn't be a surprise if they come over here to do their business. Especially considering that the toilet in the house where the tables are is on the first floor, and you have to climb a wide staircase with no railing to get there. Both houses belong to the same family, but it's way easier over here. I spot twenty rolls of toilet paper in the cupboard, all stacked with unusual care. Whoever arranged them like that obviously has a special system. I haven't got a clue how I'm going to get myself out of this one, how I'm going to slip out into the crowd, soaking wet, with a stray heater under my arm. It'll be ages until it's dark. How am I going to hide? I can't make it out the window, and I don't dare try the door. Then again, I think, I could shoot down the hallway, take a left into the bedroom, and then jump out the window into the yard, on the side of the house. It's doable, as long as I don't run into anyone. I've got to try something, because a minute ago someone knocked and tried the doorhandle. I put my shoes on, tightened the belt on my trousers, and flattened my waterlogged shirt with my hand. Interestingly, the wilted sprig of rosemary they'd pinned to my shirt a few hours ago had now perked up, its pointy narrow leaves having regained their colour with all the water. Alright then: I'm at the door, heater under my arm. Ready, steady, go. Someone's calling me. It's my father. He's standing out in the yard and has called my name twice already. It suddenly dawns on me that they might be out looking for me, that they might think something terrible has happened. His voice cuts through the cheer and commotion, slamming into my skull like a white-hot dagger. I sobered up at the speed of light. Not out of fear, but more out of shame, at the impossibility of ever being able to explain the whole caper, of anyone ever making sense of it. It'll be years, decades, before I confide in anyone. But now, standing at his hospital bedside, with an uncannily distinct memory of a single photo, the wedding and everything that happened that afternoon, I know I'll never tell anyone a thing about it.

*

The city where I live is home to a major port, the biggest in the country. Ships carry containers of every colour, all packed and sealed tight. Last year the papers were full of stories about a blue one bearing the enigmatic name MAERSK, which was detained in port for months because they'd lost its paperwork. They towed it off to the end of the breakwater, where I'd gaze out at it from my window, slowly adopting it as my own. And now, at this very moment, I think of that container as me. My paperwork's been lost, and the deadline for breaking the customs seal has come and gone. Its drunken interior, the fear, the nausea, even the light into which I'll finally emerge, they're mine alone, mine forever.

And I can't now, or ever, share this with you, Dad.

I ran out into the hallway. Seeing my father standing in the front doorway, I tore off towards him, dragging the heater cable behind me. Wet as I was, I threw my arms around him, and he kissed me.

'Where ya been?' he asked.

'I've been here,' I replied.

'C'mon, come and eat, c'mon.'

'In a sec,' I replied, and set off down the side of the house, scampering towards the low boundary wall that I intended to jump before disappearing into the surrounding woods. He didn't ask me anything, wasn't angry or worried. From that very moment, I've kept that feeling of love and kinship as my greatest, and perhaps only treasure.

I jumped, ran for it. I left the heater in a sunny meadow, so it would dry out and I could take it back tomorrow. Then I hurried off towards Grandad's house, every step shooting pain into my temples and nausea into my stomach.

I ran in my slippery, borrowed gondolas, which were so soaked and swollen that they threw me out. It was as if I'd been squishing living creatures, giant leathery snails without their shells. That's what they'd sounded like anyway.

More shots. Jole's firing up over the house at the big ceramic plates on the power poles. He hasn't yet worked it out that the precision of his salvo might soon leave the wedding guests in the dark. There was no one in the house, so I undressed in the kitchen, then went to my bedroom and put on my everyday summer clothes: cut-off jeans, sandals, a light-blue t-shirt with a panorama of Primošten on the front. And then I headed back to the wedding. I was hungry, tired. Soon I'll be sitting next to my nana, on a long bench with no backrest, and she'll be using her hands to reach over and grab me a few bits of roast meat from a metal tray. And finally, I'll get to eat, to be present at the wedding, minus the doubled-images that float and fuse, that shake like an earthquake every time I blink.

She'd arrived with a small black bag, just a handful of things inside. In the front pocket she'd slipped an envelope containing some black and white photos. She never took this sort of thing with her. They'd lain scattered in the second drawer under the television for decades. Why now? Had he asked for them? Hardly. His wants are so simple. He just wants oxygen. It's a bit off to even consider anything else. Yet sitting at his bedside, gazing out through the open window as night falls on Zagreb, I dream of days to come, of simple pleasures. Of the front porch step and flowers in blossom.

What does that crazy thing think it's doing? he'd wondered as they helped him into the ambulance on the way to the hospital. What's it doing? It's still too cold. If it's come early just to cheer me up, then sorry, but I can't take responsibility for what happens. Just wait. It won't be my fault when the frost comes for your petals. I asked you nicely, what do you think you're up to? It's still too soon. Or are you trying to tell me something, that it's too late for anything else? That I won't ever be back to see your white shirt dancing in the breeze from the field, the buzzing and chirping soon to arrive. If you're warning me, forget it. My own body is my gravest and most terrifying warning.

The darkness stretches out so far, it's indescribable. And in that darkness and sleeplessness, as the battle for oxygen rages, there are moments I surrender and moments I resolve to hope, all in the same second. You're a crazy old tree. What do you want me to do with your blossom?

I speak in his place, filling the moments until the nurse escorts us from the room.

'From tomorrow,' she says, 'from tomorrow you can't visit anymore, because of the pandemic. New regulations.'

'Nurse, we have to come,' my mother says, 'we can't just leave him here on his own.' Closing the door with her elbow on her way out, the nurse replies:

'You can come up to the hospital, but you can't be in the room with him.'

Then she pauses, opening her mouth to say something else. At that moment, I went numb, bracing myself for that old favourite about how we're all born alone, but she hesitated and then left. The spectre of birth and loneliness would have been cruel at a time like this. Punctured by lights, night's flag flickers in front of me, the city rumbling softly outside, while my father, calmed by the drugs, closes his eyes. He'll fall asleep, and we need to leave him. As he drifts off, the nurse will come and bind his arms to the bed. So he doesn't remove the mask. We all depend on that now. On fractured sleep. On the third floor, the torment of the night has begun, a stone's throw from the branches on which the city's crows take their rest.

'Why did you bring those pictures?' I ask Mum casually as we get in the car.

'I just wanted to. Does it bother you?' she replies, almost panicked.

'No, no.'

'It's good to have them here, maybe he'll want to look at them.'

'Dad?'

'Yes. When we get home, we'll pick a few out and take them up to him tomorrow, to have a look.'

'But they're just old pictures, there's nothing worth looking at.'

'Course there is, course there is.' Then she started to cry.

Turning out onto the main road, I blasted the horn at an innocent taxi driver, which at least momentarily helped me stem the waves of sorrow that had overcome my mother.

'Did we hit something?' she asks, flinching.

'No, we didn't.'

'Did someone hit us?'

'They didn't.'

'Thank God.'

I don't often have anything to say after that, and she's been saying it a lot lately.

'I'll go through them; you don't have to. The pictures, I mean.'

'Okay.'

I lie on the bed and stare at the picture from the wedding. I'd like a glass of wine in one of those tall dark-grey glasses my mother bought at the department store and kept in the village, a complete set with a sturdy jug for the wine. I'd passed whole summers in those thick grey glasses. They'd protected me from the flash of the camera and the touch and lips of unknown others. They were supposed to be reserved for special occasions, for guests, but to my brother and I, they belonged to us. From them we drank everything from watered-down wine to lemonade, and on the good days, Cedevita. Inside them I hid from every fear, from every surge of childhood sorrow, disappearing behind their grey glass. They were a good hiding place. You just needed to close your eyes, figure out what to do with your fingertips, and then let yourself drift off. But at this moment, I want my eyes wide open, to fix my gaze on my father, next to the car, with rosemary in his lapel. I want to enter that very moment, but I can't.

'Do you think he's asleep? Is he in pain?'

Mum's come to the doorway of my room and is asking me.

'He's asleep, he has to be. He's tired,' I reply, trying to reassure her, as always.

Lies are beautiful. They make life possible.

I'll take this photo up to show him tomorrow. I'll sit down at his bedside and ask him about it, see whether he remembers anything, or if he can explain how they got it. Did Jole Rocket send it over from Canada, or did he have it developed here by the local photographer, the guy who'd shown up at our place on a scorching day the previous summer, a bag slung over his shoulders, his shirt open and sweat dripping from his brow. Most likely scared of the dog we didn't have, he'd yelled from the gate: 'Photos, all your photos, weddings, funerals, first communions!'

We were sitting in the shade of the mulberry tree listening to the radio, the midday news having just begun. My grandad always listened to it before taking himself off for a lie down. In the summertime, his day began at four in the morning.

'Here you go, boss, have a look.'

On a small plastic table, the photographer set out a bunch of retouched photos, children, old folk, children, even a few group photos where he'd used a ballpoint pen to draw outlines around everyone's eyes and coated their faces in sepia, to increase the contrast. The pictures looked like they'd been taken in a circus. Posing for God knows who, these poor people had become dead clowns, playthings in the hands of a provincial hawker, who reckoned that he'd breathed new life into them. When my grandad saw the people in the pictures, he almost shuddered.

'We don't want any,' he said.

'That'd be a crying shame,' the photographer shot back, 'these are so much better, and they're not even expensive, c'mon, show me your pictures, I'll take photos of them and bring them back in a month's time, all done. For you, boss, just for you, I'll do the wedding photos for free...'

'No thanks, no need,' Grandad replied.

Yasser Arafat was saying something on the transistor radio, a Sanyo, but the photographer wouldn't quit.

'Let me do a few, c'mon, you don't wanna be the village cheapskate.'

'I do actually,' replied my grandad, almost peevish now. 'Are you hungry?'

'No, boss, I'm not.'

'Are you thirsty?'

'I could manage a drink.'

Grandad went to the cellar and decanted some wine into a green glass bottle, stuffed a cork in it, then filled half a wooden mug with red wine, adding cold water from the faucet in the yard.

'Here you go, drink up, and be on your way. Thanks, but we don't want any photos.'

Then he slid the bottle in the bloke's bag, picked the transistor up from the table, and went to his room to lie down. I was left standing there alone as the bloke tipped up the mug and chugged down the watery wine.

'Would you like some more?' I asked him.

'Wouldn't hurt.'

I went to the cellar and poured another half a glass. Just as I was about to turn the faucet on, he put his hand on mine,

'No need, boy, shame to spoil it.'

He drained the mug, gathered up his pictures and started cursing.

'Why are you saying swearwords?' I asked, not knowing where that came from.

The crickets were hard at it on their flaming violins, the air trembling in the heat.

'And you can go fuck yourself too,' the photographer replied, half-drunk.

He got his pictures together, slung his bag over his shoulder, and headed towards the gate. I was fuming, but didn't say anything. All of a sudden, there at our gate, the guy yelped and grabbed the back of his head where his hair was drenched in sweat, blood running through his fingers. Someone had fired a slingshot and managed a direct hit, ending the visit. The bloke wouldn't dare come back. I turned around, hoping to catch a glimpse of the shooter. But in the sweltering summer cacophony, neither man nor beast moved. I went to the gate and tipped a bucket of water over the drops of blood, washing it all away. I stood there in the sun, watering the stains, savouring a moment of unexpected vengeance. Then my neighbour Pere came down from the upper terrace, a powerful slingshot in hand. He was twenty years old and pretty useless with a slingshot. But today he'd managed to hit his target, and that was as good as it gets. He's as thick as pigshit, but he's pretty as an angel, that's what his grandma had said, a sharp-tongued old battle-axe who let her sheep sleep in the house.

In the end, what does it matter who developed the photo? Why am I sifting through a time so far away, a moment that has already frozen and petrified, like a snail fossil in a stone among the billions of other stones that line the shore. I'd like to say a word in my defence, but at the same time, I don't. I want to cherish every second that remains to us, that's what I want to tell you when I see the duty nurse posting a notice on the door to the corridor leading to your room, banning patient visits because of the pandemic. Do you even know anything about Covid-19, that terrifying new word that now separates us? That has erected a wall between us at the very time when we should be tearing all our old walls down. When the only thing that matters now is the love we have for each other, the love we can show each other in the time left to steal.

'I'm going to bed,' says my mother. 'I'll take a taxi up in the morning, and when you come home from work, we can head back up together.'

'I don't know if they'll let you in,' I say.

'I have to go, you that know that, I'll ask for five minutes with him, just five minutes. I'm going to ring him now, see if he's asleep.'

She went to her room and closed the door, but I see her, I can see the whole thing. She's hunched over, mobile phone pressed to her ear, and when he picks up at the other end, she speaks loudly and slowly, over-enunciating. So he gets the message, so he understands that we're going to try and come and see him, that we're going to take him home, that we're going to save his life, which can't be saved. He tries to reply through the mask, but his words barely carry to her. She listens to the squeaky whistle of air, him saying something she can't understand. At least we managed to hear each other's voices, that's what she'll say later.

Two shots ring out in the night and give me the fright of my life. Then I realise that it's just someone celebrating a Croatian goal in a friendly against Lithuania. You'd have to be a fucking dick to pull out a pistol when a ball rolls into a net. But that's clearly a minority view, because others in the neighbourhood respond with firecrackers and cheers. We quiet folk, we just keep quiet. Our team's leading, they're playing superbly, they're going to win. We've got nothing to complain about.

Jole Rocket grew old in Canada. He's out there on his glazed porch waiting to die, no chance of ever giving it both barrels, which was his phrase for firing a shotgun. Boom boom. But if he were here now, he'd definitely reply, the dipshit to whom I owe so much. His passion for shooting created this photo, but I still don't understand why he took it. What did he see in the man leaning on the bonnet of a second-hand Fiat, hair parted to the side, a digital Seiko on his wrist? Why did the man gaze so happily towards the Pentax, and how is it, that at that very moment, a dipshit like Jole managed to press the shutter and create an image like this? As a child, I'd spend hours flicking through our photos, but I'd always pause at this one, an image of happiness itself, a man who is calm, collected, silent, and happy. It's extraordinary, the role crazy Jole Rocket played in our lives, at least in mine, and at least tonight.

They've started to restrain him so he doesn't get out of bed and take the mask off, and then fall and hurt himself due to a lack of oxygen. 'Why don't they give him something to help him sleep?' I asked the nurse as she passed me in the corridor today.

'You'd have to ask the doctor,' she said, gently fobbing me off.

I asked the first doctor I met on the ward.

'We can't, he's weak.'

'You don't think he'll wake up,' I said, staring at her, not expecting an answer.

She just shrugged her shoulders and kept walking. At that moment, every bone and muscle in my body went limp and my temples started to pound. Yes, that's all I needed to know. The torment. The hopelessness.

Is he sleeping, is he lying there having spasms, what's he thinking about?

I was again twelve years old when I set off to bring our horse and cow in from the back meadow. They're chained to steel posts driven deep into the ground, and I need to bring them home, water them, and milk the cow. My father wants to come along. Let's go for a walk, he says. I'm confused, because when we're together, we do real jobs, like concreting and stuff, we don't do easy stuff like going for walks. Never. Even when my brother and I go for a swim, we run the hundred meters or so from the car to the beach by ourselves. I'd never been for a walk with my father, this was the first time. I remember a few of the things we talked about. I asked him what the path we were on looked like when he was a boy. It was a forest, he said, full of rabbits and partridges. As we walk, the sun falls behind us, sinking down beneath the cypresses next to the church, the dappled light filtering through their darkness, the odd ray dancing along the rough surface of the trunk, bringing another summer's day to a silent close. But until that happens, in the gloaming, as a golden glow streams out over the fields and vineyards, as we bask in the gentle warmth on the backs of our necks, and little dust clouds rise at our feet, the day isn't yet done. There's enough time to bring the animals home before first dark, when the woman who brings her bottles to buy milk from my grandma will arrive.

We soon came out onto a long, broad meadow. The cow was chewing its cud, the horse still grazing, lifting and then lowering its head as it saw us, monumental and white like a sculpture, only the thinnest of chains around its powerful neck and thick, almost mustard-coloured mane. Both animals are so calm, so harmless. Dad untied the cow, and she waddled over to a patch of grass she hadn't been able to reach. I untied the horse, and he tore off, rearing up on his hind legs in unbridled joy. As we strolled across the dry grass as if it were carpet, my father first knelt down, and then lay on his stomach. I did the same, our foreheads almost touching.

This man of thirty-seven, a master baker and house builder, then patted the grass with his open palm, and butterflies and gnats soon took flight. Then he did the same with his other hand. And then I did it, and then him again, smiling, radiant. He only said: 'Gorgeous, isn't it? What more could one want?' Just the butterflies in a field at dusk, just the butterflies and their quiet, eternal hum.

But I couldn't speak, I could only lie there soaking up this sudden intimacy, the horse standing over me as I rolled onto my back. From below, I stared up at the under side of his belly, neck, and head. He bent down a little, looked me in the eye, snorted, and walked off.

'Shall we go,' my father said, bringing me back into the world. He'd already pulled out the stakes, bundled up the chain, and hidden them in a thorn bush next to the sledgehammer I'd use again tomorrow. We walked slowly, trailing behind the horse and cow, both still so calm as the sun made its way around the cypresses. At the edge of the meadow, I clambered up onto a dry stone wall and mounted the horse. My father took a few quick strides, grabbed its mane, and leapt up in front of me onto the horse's back, like an Indian. We rode slowly, following the cow as it ambled down the shadowy path.

Covered in sweat, I turned over in bed. I got up, stood at the window, and gazed out at the headlights, an enormous billboard flashing on the roof of the building nextdoor. Should I tell him all this tomorrow? That I remember? Or would that be wrong? There's no time for collecting memories anymore, the sediment has broken the bottle, and fresh soil now lies piled ready next to my father, the man who spoke with butterflies I didn't even know existed.

I'm going to get my phone and search up anything I can find about flour causing lung disease. It's haunting me. My whole life long, I've never touched anything softer than flour.

Is is even possible, or was the doctor just making up stories, hoping to impress his colleague and the nurse. Or does the mighty hand of death lurk in that fine grind, the hand that first pressed on my father's lungs a few years ago, deciding to regulate his oxygen here on earth. Did the flour really do it? Or was it fate? Is he sleeping? Is his night restful? I'm afraid of the answer to that question.

II

SKENDER AND his four sons arrived four days ago. They sleep in a truck down by the house of the Italian my father calls Signor Fascist. In a white skullcap, Skender had knocked at the door one afternoon, and Mum had invited him in. He took his shoes off, entered the hallway, and then seemed to bow. I was standing behind my mother. I'd seen people in caps like this before. They're Muslims. They often came to our neighbourhood to visit their children. They always went about in jackets and long dark trousers, always wearing those caps, even when the sun had melted the asphalt and high summer was blowing its golden trumpet at full blast. Our house was the only one without a façade. It was pretty, compact, and still red, even though the bricks had been bled by salt carried on the northeaster and the endless rain had blackened their edges with a fine moss, like patches of smog. I was ashamed of it. There were houses in our street that didn't have proper roofs, just a concrete slab with steel rebar stakes sticking up in the corners and a stack of bricks waiting to become a new floor. Even if it was only a thin layer of plaster painted white, nothing fancy, they still had a façade. But we didn't even have that. Our house was built on a steep slope on the edge of a karst sinkhole. On one side it had three floors and was almost nine metres high. It looked like it might topple over. Seen from the street, it was a single storey. Skender and his sons were from Gostivar and façades were their speciality, especially the most durable and expensive kind: *Terrebonne.* I remember it. Skender would roll the 'r' sound as if it were stuck at the top of his trachea, slinking from the openness of the neighbouring vowels. He'd seen that we didn't have a façade and had wanted to offer us this very *terrebonne.* He and his sons had been away from home for two months now, and in that time, they'd finished ten façades, added a handful of floors, and built five garages. That's what he told us.

'And next up, boss, how 'bout we sort you out? All work guaranteed,' he added solemnly, as if swearing an oath. His back to the window, my father sat at the table smoking. Skender joined him.

'Would you like coffee?' my mother asked.

'No thanks, Ma'am.'

'How about a shot of slivovitz?' my father suddenly remembered.

'We don't drink, we're Muslims. It's not our custom.'

'At least have something,' my mother said, laying some wafers out on a small crystal plate and placing it in front of him.

'No thanks, Ma'am. Don't want to put you to any bother.'

'How much would it cost me?' my father asked.

'You're a good man, gotta coupla boys. I'll do you a discount.'

'How do you know that?' my mother interrupted, breaking into a smile.

Skender didn't answer, just stubbed out his cigarette, looked at my father, and said:

'I've been this way a few times, been to the store, the kiosk, got a handle on the place. Good people.'

'Alright then, do your calculations. Measure up the house and we'll see how we go.'

'Nothing to measure,' Skender replied. 'House is eight by ten, floors are two metres eighty. Don't you worry, boss, I won't rip you off,' he said in an almost exalted tone. 'I've got four brothers and we all do façades. No tricks.'

Then he said a figure that I immediately forgot, but I saw my father put his hand over his mouth, tilting his head to the side a little, while Mum let out a sigh.

'We don't have that kind of money,' she said.

'It's *terrebonne*, Ma'am, it lasts a hundred years. We could do roughcast, or something else, but it's not worth it.'

'Would you sleep and eat here with us?' she asked.

'Ma'am, that's not your worry.'

'And if we decided to go for it, when could you start?'

'Tomorrow, Ma'am. Six days and we're done, if it doesn't rain.'

My father stood up, went over to the window and opened the curtains. Our tenant had just parked his new Citroën Pallas in front of the garage, where our old Fiat sat waiting for one of its rare outings.

He turned around, offered Skender his hand, and said:

'You can start tomorrow, if you've got the men.'

'Got my sons, boss, my sons,' Skender replied, having sprung to his feet to shake my father's hand.

I get myself ready to head up to the hospital. I've got a meeting with Dad's doctor at eleven. She's asked me to come alone, without Mum. You can tell her about it later, it's just that we can't have hordes of people here at the moment, she'd said. Mum had phoned him this morning. He hadn't answered. So half an hour later, she rang him another three times, and in the hour that followed, three times more. It was only then that he picked up, almost incoherent, barely able to string a sentence together, his thoughts swirling somewhere in the pockets without oxygen, the connections between them having burst like soap bubbles. He's alive, Mum said, that's the main thing. He's alive.

This morning we looked at the photos she'd brought, flicking through the black and white images in near silence. Anxious and afraid, she then arranged them by size, biggest at the bottom, smallest on top, ones for documents, his and hers. Two beautiful, young people with totally different features, complexions, everything. Two foreigners from opposite ends of the earth: he fair-haired, blue-eyed, and round-faced, she dark-haired, brown-eyed, with sculpted cheekbones and a sharp nose. Yet there in front of the camera, at a photo studio across the road from the police station where they'd submitted their applications for ID cards and passports, you sense a hint of fear in them.

She's sitting next to me as I drive, having insisted that she come along. She's bought a bread roll, a banana (for the calcium), water, a little tub of cottage cheese, and some yogurt. Even when he's at home he doesn't eat, she explains.

'But they won't let you in, Mum. They're going to close all the hospitals, because of the virus. They've been talking about it for days.'

'We'll see,' she replies. 'I'll ask the nurse if I can nip in. What does he care about the virus?' She's trying to placate me, wanting me to accept her recalcitrance.

'Fine. When I'm with the doctor, you wait for me out in the corridor.'

'Look, we're going to take your father off the drugs. He's taking a heap of them, but they're not making any difference...'
'Okay.'
'I'm sorry, I really am, but he's stage four, end-stage...'

I was nodding so frantically that I interrupted her, forcing her to shrink back behind her laptop screen.

'Sorry, doctor, I know what you're saying, I really do, but I need a favour, a big one, gigantic.'

'What is it? You know we'll do anything we can.'

'I know, and I'm very grateful.' My throat tightened and I went quiet for a moment. Then I said that we'd like to take him home. 'It's all he wants.'

'I know, he told us that too. But he can't travel, you know that, he needs 15 litres of oxygen an hour. How far is home?' she asked.

'Three hours.'

'That's 45 litres. The ambulance doesn't have a bottle that size. It'd have to be ordered in especially.'

'Okay, who takes care of that?'

'It's big risk, you know that.'

'I'll sign anything. Better he dies in the ambulance than in here. At least then he'll know he was on his way home. Do you know what I mean?'

'Very much so. I had a similar situation in my own family.'

'So we understand each other. As soon as possible then?'

'I have to talk to my supervisor. But yes, we'll get the ball rolling. I'm sorry, I really am…'

'You've done so much, doctor. I'm very grateful.'

I went out into the corridor, a smile ready for Mum, but she wasn't there. I knew she'd gone up to the room to see him. I bounded up the stairs, snuck past two workers coming back from a cigarette break, sweat and nicotine radiating in their wake. Upstairs, the corridor was deserted. The no visiting rule is all over the newspapers, but here there's just a scrap of paper with a single sentence. The doors are locked, but that's no change. A nurse came by carrying a small metal tray with some tablets, and as she opened the door to Dad's room, I saw him. He looked exhausted. Mum was feeding him with a spoon, lifting and lowering the mask, smiling the unwavering smile of a little girl full of hope, enjoying this moment of togetherness. Dad sees me and raises his hand, blue with bruising from the cannula. I start doing the numbers. How many more times will he raise his hand? How many? I take my phone out and wave. He waves back, and I take a picture.

Skender and his sons had parked their truck on the unsealed edge of the narrow road on which we lived. Cut into the hard stone, the street wound its way between houses with barrel kennels in the front yard. The dogs, chained to trees or wedges driven in the stone, didn't often use their kennels, which were like furnaces in summer and ice boxes in winter. They preferred to sleep outside, another of life's absurdities in a working-class neighbourhood. A lucky few had wooden kennels raised up on blocks, which meant that they didn't flood when the torrents of rain surged down the slope. The dogs were vicious mutts. And now, as their owners trudged up the hill, heading home from work at the port or the factory, they had to squeeze past a truck belonging to some bloody Albanians from out of town. Skender didn't care what people thought of them. He was a master tradesman, a dignified and serious man, which is how he carried himself. His sons silently unloaded the steel pipes and thick wooden planks, stacking them neatly, before piling the couplings into a wheelbarrow and wheeling them into our yard, where the youngest, who I'd later learn was called Škeljzen, greased them with motor oil to make everything easier to screw together. When the truck was finally empty, under his father's watchful eye, one of the sons jumped in the cab and drove the truck back down to where the road widened a little. As people ambled past the truck, no one dared say a word. Skender just stood there with his sleeves rolled up, a strange-looking implement in his powerful arms. It looked like a hoe, but it was bigger and more unwieldy, its handle at least two metres long. Today they were going to put the scaffold up on the front of the house. Tomorrow they'd do the façade. Then they'd dismantle the whole thing and reassemble it on the other side, the high one, along the edge of the sinkhole.

    I could see Dad talking to Skender out on the terrace. Chesterfields, they're good, he said, offering him a cigarette. When Skender headed off to bolt the scaffolding together with his giant spanner, Dad practically ran inside to tell Mum that Skender had been in the army in Zadar and that he knew the area well.

'How old is he?' Mum asked.

'Don't know, about the same as me. But they marry at fifteen or sixteen, and then they have heaps of kids.'

It was a Monday, and when I got back from school, the scaffolding was almost up. I ducked under the planks and went inside. Mum and Dad were sitting at the table, having just had lunch.

'Son, did you know that your father and I are going to get married?'

'You're already married, aren't you?'

'We are, but we're not in church, so we thought… We've been to see Father Ante, he's going to marry us on Friday, at four.'

'That's good. Who'll be the witnesses?'

'Your aunt and uncle, if we need them.'

'We couldn't do it when we were younger. You know yourself how bloody poor we were. The day we got married, we came home from work, washed up, gunned it to the registry, and an hour later we were circling pickaxes and sledgehammers, digging the foundations for the house.'

'I know all that, you already told me. And Mum was scared that you'd miss.'

'I still worry about that darling,' she said with a smile.

'It's a great idea, go for it,' I said.

'But how're we going to manage with this lot here?' Mum asked herself, as if there'd ever been peace in our house.

If it wasn't the workmen or the three tenant families on the lower floors needing something, then the neighbours would be over asking for wine or slivovitz. Every summer we'd buy a few tonnes of watermelon, a whole truckful, and unload them in the front yard. On their way home, people would buy melons in every shade of green, carting them up the hill, past their thirsty, yappy mutts.

'Albos are good people,' said my father. 'There was one in the army with me. He couldn't talk, but boy he could make a loaf of bread.'

My father was a baker in the army too. He didn't have a rifle, didn't even go to target practice, nothing. A solder in white slippers and clean white trousers.

I went to my room and lay down on the low narrow bed. On the floor, beside the headboard, there was a stack of books and comics, a box of Neapolitan wafers, and a red lamp made out of metal so thin that it fell over every time you touched the switch. With the lamp lying on its side, the bulb shone right in my eyes instead of the river Ken Parker was descending on his raft. I didn't really own anything of any value. Not unless you count my thick double-breasted cardigan with its waistbelt, collar, and two front pockets, the whole thing stretching down to my thighs. My mother knitted it as an upgrade on a spring or autumn jacket if I had to go somewhere with school. As a family, we only went to the village, to Nana and Grandad's. Lying there with a wafer in my mouth and a second balanced on my forehead (so I didn't have to reach over and disturb my afternoon slumber), it occurred to me that someone was going to need to take photos at the wedding. My parents definitely wouldn't remember. I got up. My brother and I kept our stuff in the sideboard, in the place for the drinks. He had his wagons and Indians, and I had my favourite book, *White Fang*. I'd borrowed it from the school library and had decided that I wasn't going to return it. Mrs Vukušić was nice about my overdue book at first, but later, her tone sharpened. 'You've had *White Fang* for two months now. You have to bring it back.' 'I will,' I replied softly, heading for the door. 'Where are you going?' 'To class. I just remembered something.' That was the end of my trips to the library, which I adored. I'd cover a big round table with atlases, encyclopaedias, dictionaries, all the books we weren't allowed to take out. I'd pore over them for hours. By the time I went home, I'd know everything about the habits of the Eurasian blue tit, the course of the Tigris, the economy of the American Midwest, and the ocean currents around Hawaii. I even knew that when the Vikings drank mead from the skulls of their slaughtered foes, they'd make a toast: *Skål!*

But that was a bridge too far for me, and so was returning *White Fang*. I had a plan, but I was too chicken to try it. One day I'd give it a go, but until then, I wasn't returning the book, no way. I've been there and I've cried icy tears over every word. Miners of gold, compared to me, you're the damned of the earth. That's what I'd thought as I held the book's sellotaped spine in my hands. My first plan was to go up to Mrs

Vukušić and say that I'd lost the book and that I'd pay the fine. But how could I lie about something like this? And my other plan was to front up and tell her that I love the book and that I want to keep it. You can want whatever you like, but others want to read it too, that's what she'll probably reply. And then I wouldn't know what to do, because I'm only in year five. I'd have to carry the shame for another three years. That was it, I wasn't going to do anything. I'd sit tight and play for time. Maybe she'll go on maternity leave and forget about it. I once overheard one of mother's friends talking about how after she gave birth she became a total budgie brain. That could happen to Mrs Vukušić, she's good-natured, she might just forget about it.

Besides the book, my other treasure is the camera that my aunt brought me from Switzerland. It was a beautifully designed, idiot-proof Kodak, and it came complete with a black plastic case, a wrist strap, a set of twelve flashes, and two rolls of film. What a dream! My brother and I spent a lot of time staring at it, but hadn't dared try it out. Who should we ask to insert the film? I only knew that the strip can't be exposed to the light. We once tried fiddling with it in the pitch dark, but with no luck. I don't even know how you put the battery in, how you wind the film on (or does it do that automatically?), or how you take it out. There were so many times when I'd wanted to take photos of the ships in the bay as they waited for their turn to dock and unload. One time, an American warship had sailed into the shipyard for repairs, its artillery cannons so big that you could see them from our balcony.

Today was Monday, and I had until Friday to figure out how it all worked, so I could take photos in the church at my parents' wedding. I'm a bit shy, but tomorrow I'll pack the Kodak in my schoolbag and take it to the woodwork teacher to have a look. I don't know anyone else who could help. I've seen a few old cameras on the shelf in his den, which is what he calls the little room down the back of the classroom where he hangs out with one of the PE teachers, smoking and drinking and talking. He'd once sent me to the shop to buy two litres of red wine. Buy yourself some biscuits, he'd said. But I didn't. I gave him the change and the receipt. I'd loved that he'd picked me to fetch something so important. He knew that I wouldn't blab, that I sold wine and slivovitz from barrels in our garage, and that I knew about alcohol and its wonders. He moonlighted making chess pieces on the lathe, went mad when we used the saws around the wrong way, but I was sure that he was the best person to give me a few tips about photography. No one in my family had any idea.

I'd finished the wafer that was balancing on my forehead and was now lying in semi-darkness, staring out the window from my position in the lowlands. Although it was starting to get dark, I could almost make out a face, a young guy putting up the scaffolding. He waved and smiled shyly. I jumped out of bed, opened the window, and told him my name. He told me his, and then quickly shuffled off, heavy pipes trailing behind him, the four couplings hanging from his waist almost pulling his pants down. It was the youngest son. Škeljzen.

We were sitting on red plastic chairs in the same corridor, waiting for his door to open, hoping to at least catch a glimpse of him, see whether he was sleeping, breathing, or if he was still even there. He'd been given a roommate, a guy about my age with teeth as black as coal. It was the drugs, he'd told my mother when she'd glanced over at him. Like that meant anything to her. We knew as much about drugs as we knew about the Kodak I'd taken to the woodwork teacher. And now I'm dying, Lucky explained. We could see that too. But maybe he would be able to help Dad during the nights, make him feel less alone. On the other hand, it's also possible that he'd go psycho and murder him. He certainly looked capable of it. Our shoulders touching, my mother and I sat there warming each other, just like those two terrifying and contradictory thoughts.

'What are we waiting for?' I ask her.

'I'd like to go in and sit with him for a bit. I mean, how on earth is that guy allowed in?'

A sales rep carrying an expensive briefcase had just strolled by, typing something into his mobile phone. When it rang, he'd said Azecolab and the door had opened. Azecolab. What a weird code word for freedom.

'We're not allowed in though. That's not right.'

'I won't be in anyone's way,' Mum protested, 'they're letting everyone else in.'

She had a point. If Azecolab opened doors, why wouldn't they let a worried old woman in. She couldn't do any harm, only good. Lucky suddenly appeared in the doorway to Dad's room and was calling out for the nurse. A second later he was telling her to bring new batteries for the remote, that the old ones weren't working. As she walked away, Lucky spotted us and started shaking Dad's leg, pointing in our direction. Dad got himself up on his elbow, smiled, and signalled for us to go home, flicking the back of his hand in a gesture that was supposed to mean that neither he, nor anything to do with him, mattered anymore. It was then that I pressed the buzzer, mumbled Azecolab, and the door magically opened. We took our chance.

'You'll be going home soon, Dad.'

'Now?' He lit up.

'Not now, not tomorrow, maybe the day after. We need to figure a few things out first.'

'Alright, doesn't matter,' he replied, already out of breath.

'Do you want a banana?' Mum asked, perched on the edge of the bed, fixing his pyjamas.

'No, you go home. You're not allowed here,' he said.

'Course they are,' Lucky piped up, black teeth and all. 'Every fuckin' man and his dog are coming and going.'

'That's true. Do you need anything?' I asked him.

'Nah, my sister came by. She's not actually my real sister, she's my stepdad's daughter. Long fucking story.'

The crows are cawing in the treetops around the hospital, making a hell of a racket. It's the first time I've heard them this spring. The sound penetrates right down into my femur, shooting a sharp arrow of fear. And now that fear is turning the arrow, turning it and boring a hole.

'You have to eat,' I tell her as we drove home from the hospital.

'I can't.'

'You won't be in any state to take him anywhere. You'll collapse in the ambulance.'

That got her attention. 'Do you think they'll let him out? Don't you worry about me, I'll be fine.'

'They'll let him out. They said they will.'

That's where I left it, worn out by the constant hoping against hope, the pain in my thigh now excruciating. I drove slowly, not trusting myself to put it into third and accelerate. What if the crows caw, what if I hear that bone-chilling sound declaring victory over everything – the moment, the twilight, this exhausted hope? In the face of this, and in the face of everything else that's happening, I have to remain humiliatingly meek. That is now the measure of all things. Helplessness. Low expectations. To die in one's own home. I say the sentence aloud, emphasising *home*. I hurriedly whisper *to die*. Maybe it won't come to that.

But my leg hurts more than ever.

It was pouring down when I ran to school. I'd barely made it out the front door before the southerly had wrecked my umbrella. I tossed it up on the half-assembled scaffold, the workers huddling underneath, waiting for the rain to stop. As soon as it did, they'd be back up connecting everything that they'd be taking down the day after tomorrow. I tore straight through the puddles, thinking I'd dry off in class. One of the girls who sits next to the radiator will swap places with me. I'll sit there in bare feet the whole lesson long, my shoes and socks tucked neatly under the heating pipes. I had the Kodak in my satchel, wrapped in a plastic bag, and had shoved a bottle of wine down next to my books, having first wrapped it in newspaper. I'd taken the page with the death notices. Fascinating that I always manage that. The neighbours had once asked me to pick up the bones from the two suckling pigs they'd roasted at one of their parties. I brought some old newspaper for the job, and when I got home, our dog ended up feasting on pork crackling from the death notices. When Mum saw it, she quickly looked the other way. I didn't pay any attention at the time, but now I think I'd find it funny. To avoid carting the greasy paper to the rubbish bin, I put a match to it where we normally burned branches and dry leaves from the garden. Something savage crackled in the flames. Maybe it was the grease. Maybe it was something else.

At lunchtime I headed for the den. Mr Pavlić was sitting in a cloud of cigarette smoke, staring at the wall. He hadn't heard me knock and jumped a little when I came in. I got straight to it, told him I needed his help, told him everything. He just grinned. His eyes were bloodshot, and his thin frame was somehow bloated. When he stood up, his head slumped over to one side. Is he drunk? He's not saying much. I think he's only just managing to hold it together. 'For a rainy day,' I say, taking the bottle wrapped in the death notices from my bag. 'Thanks, put it over there. What is it, elderflower?'

'No, it's wine, from home.'

'Aha, that's good, just as long as it's not that bullshit cordial.'

'I don't even know what elderflower is,' I reply, trying to strike up some friendly conversation.

'A bush, white flowers. My ex-girlfriend drowned me in the shit.'

'Aha, your ex.'

'Yip, dumped me yesterday, threw me out. Forget it, it's no big deal.'

'Course not, plenty of fish and all that.'

'Yep, plenty of fish and all that. Now pay attention. This is where you insert the film, and this is where you wind it on. Once you've shut it, you can take a photo. It'll go to the next picture by itself. When you finish the roll, you take the film out and that's that.'

He hands me the camera and I'm worried that I'll break something.

'You can't break it, matey. You'd have to throw it at the wall for it break.'

'Why do you say that?'

'Because that's what my missus did to me this morning. Gave me the old heave-ho.'

'Did she hit you?'

'Nah, don't worry about it. Gimme that bottle a sec. Let's see if anyone famous died.' He laughed at that. Good old Mr Pavlić. Your heart breaking for a chick, that's bullshit. A big dog lying in frozen mud, a couple of hooligans beating the crap out of it. Now that's heartbreak. But a girl, no way, that's pure bullshit. If only I'd had the courage to tell him what I was thinking.

All flustered, on the way home I kept wanting to stop somewhere, get the camera out, and point it at something. But I decided to save my firepower. A film's only got 24 shots. I'll use one cannister of film for my parents' wedding and save the other for mucking around, for taking pictures to stick on the wall above my bed. I can already see the neighbour's long, blue Ford Taunus with the sun shining on it from behind, the houses swaying in the back window, our neighbourhood flickering in the greenery. Then 23 more shots just like that one. I imagined nicking a dozen sardines from the fishmonger's barrow one Friday, laying them out in front of the neighbour's dog and letting him have a good sniff. Click. Then I'd get some cats and do something similar. Scales and fur, that's the idea. My imagination ran wild, my palms almost sweating.

Skender and his sons were almost like ghosts, silent and invisible. They prepared the *terrebonne* in a big shallow plastic tub next to the house. First the sons would tip the cement, sand, and water in, and then, as Skender added more water from a bucket, they'd mix it together with their hoes. Every so often, he'd briefly tense up, worried that there was too much water, because this meant adding more of everything else, which also meant that the new batch wouldn't be up to standard. Once the mix was up on the wall and dry, Skender didn't want any botches, by which I think he meant to say blotches. Botches didn't necessarily mean that the façade would crumble, but that would mean that he and his sons hadn't lived up to their good name. Skender was too proud to let that happen. At almost seventeen, Škeljzen was about a year older than me. But he worked just like the others. Sometimes he'd even do the heavy lifting, up there on a plank of wood, high in the air. He'd heave two enormous buckets up onto the scaffolding, full to the brim, and then hang them on hooks. Then one of his brothers would pass them on up to their father, who'd be on his knees doing the plastering, a cigarette in the corner of his mouth and a fresh white skullcap on his head. All this happened in silence. They worked fast, they had to finish a side of the house a day, stopping only briefly to eat. Skender would buy three loaves of bread and five small tins of hash from the kiosk across the road. That was lunch. He wouldn't let my mother cook for them, wouldn't even let her heat up the hash. But my mother knew deprivation, because she'd experienced it herself. She didn't give up.

'Hunger'll be the death of you, Skender.'

'We're not hungry, Ma'am. But thanks.'

'If pork's the problem, just say so.'

'It's not, Ma'am.'

'Then it's agreed that you'll eat here tomorrow.'

'We can't afford to lose time, Ma'am.'

'You won't be losing anything. You don't even have to wash up.'

When she turned to go, even Skender, stubborn as he was, knew that that was the end of the conversation. And he knew his sons were hungry. Watching them hauling their buckets of concrete, I thought their bones might suddenly snap and poke through their clothes, or that their eyes might burst. But none of them complained. Bar the odd word from their father in Albanian, no one said a word. They'd just nod, grimace occasionally, and get on with the job. The next day my mother made a hearty soup, prepared some salad, and roasted two chickens with potatoes. She even put some Coca Cola in the fridge. That's lunch, she figured. For us she made stuffed capsicum. I would have given everyone the stuffed capsicum, but at the butcher you could never be sure whether some pork had gotten stuck in the grinder. My father had just looked at her as she explained it all to him. He had the eyes of a man on safe footing, who didn't ever have to worry about falling, who didn't have any reason to doubt.

And so our house got its sparkling white blanket. *Terrebonne*. With every new batch, Skender would wrap a sheet of glass in an old rag, smash it to pieces, and then toss the little diamonds in the mix. 'Now it'll shine in the sun,' he explained, as I looked on in wide-eyed wonder. And he was right. By Friday, when we were coming back from my parents' wedding at the church, our house glistened a magical white. 'It's good that we did it,' said my father. He meant the wedding and the rigmarole with Father Ante, not the façade. It dawned on me that from this day forward, I wasn't going to be living in a house of unrendered brick. If I wanted to invite a friend over, I wouldn't feel that lump of shame in my throat, that knot that made me feel so alone.

'So we'll know tomorrow then?' my mother asks as I fry a few eggs for dinner.

She doesn't want anything to eat. But I'm my mother's son, and I badger her until she relents, just like she badgered Skender.

'You have to have at least one. And a little cheese, and some yogurt.'

'I can't manage all that.'

'You have to eat something.'

'We'll know tomorrow then?' she says, repeating herself.

'I don't know. I have to call the doctor, then we'll know.'

'Don't call her, go and see her. We'll go together. I want to race in and see your father.'

'You can't do that, Mum. We're in a pandemic, the whole world's gone crazy.'

'I'll sneak in. I won't be the only one. I'll just duck in and out. It's not like I'll be wandering around the ward like that criminal.'

'What criminal?'

'You know, the tall one, the guy who ran over those two Belgians in his speedboat.'

'They were Italian.'

'That's them, they were in a sailboat.'

'What was he doing at the hospital?'

'No idea, just lurking in the corridor, talking to people.'

'Alright then, we'll do that. We'll go around ten, when they've finished their rounds.'

'Better that we go around nine. It'll take us a while to get there. Better to get there early and wait.'

'Okay.'

How can I refuse her, I thought to myself. How can I refuse such a need.

'Škeljzen!' Skender shouted, before following it with something terse in Albanian. He'd caught his youngest son in our garage, kneeling down beside the big wine barrel, shelling almonds with the quick tap of his hammer, before scoffing them. Hearing his father's voice, he jumped to his feet, dropping the hammer on the concrete floor. I was reclining in the front seat of our Fiat, the requests show on the car radio playing Bob

Dylan. It looked like Skender was going to murder his son and that I'd be the only witness, so I leapt out and ran next to Škeljzen.

'He was doing it for me, Mister Skender, I'm useless with a hammer. He was doing it for me…'

'Don't you dare steal!'

'He wasn't stealing,' I protested.

'Shut up, young fella,' Skender said, cutting me off. And I did indeed shut up. For a second or two, Skender just stood there, eyeballing us, wondering what to do. He gave a gruff command, and Škeljzen, relieved, knelt back down, grabbed a brush, swept the shells into his hand, and scurried off out the garage door. He returned a little later, looked over to me, and waved. That was thank you. I climbed back in the car and turned the radio up. On the verge of bawling the anguished tears that had welled up inside me, I started changing the gears with the car still off, trying to forget.

We were all set for three o'clock this afternoon. It was now eight in the morning and my brother was still asleep. Dad had come home from his shift at six. Mum wasn't going to work. The dog had taken off somewhere last night, but he'd come back when he's tired and hungry. There aren't many cars around here, and nothing poisonous. The dog can handle everything else. When Dad heads off to work each night, the dog runs along behind the car barking. Then he wanders back, panting. Sometimes he doesn't come back for days, and when he finally does, it looks like he's been in a scrap. I've noticed that he never runs away on the odd night Dad has off. Those nights he just lies around on the carpet in the doorway. Black, in the dark.

The church is in the old part of our neighbourhood, maybe a couple of kilometres up the hill. It's a roomy building, with a little churchyard and a big rectory where I go for religious education. I've thought about it. I believe in God because I'm scared of death. God at least offers some kind of explanation for everything. And then there's the fact that my friends go too. One even got a cross tattooed on his right shoulder. When his dad got home from the shipyard, he almost murdered him, so my friend added a few letters to the cross. TNT. He loved Alan Ford. And he really believed in God. He was the best at singing *Kyrie eleison* and I loved listening to him. A nun taught the classes. Sometimes we watched films about Jesus, and other times we'd play football. Lately we've been doing a lot of praying, because Father Ante is trying to sort out his nicotine addiction. That devil nicotine, that's what sister calls it. At the start of each lesson, we pray for peace on earth, the Holy Father, our homeland, and Father Ante. That he may find the strength, as sister would say, staring down at the tips of her shiny black moccasins. Why would a priest smoke? I wondered. Isn't it a terrible sin to poison our God-given bodies? That's a really bad decision. I prayed loudly – lead *him* not into temptation, I'd say, adjusting that part a little. I pictured Father Ante stubbing his last cigarette out with his expensive Italian shoes, before turning his face towards a sudden beam of light as it burst through clouds the colour of tobacco smoke. Every time I went to town with Mum, I'd see his brown shoes in the Borovo department store window. Mum once bought our whole family a pair of shoes each. I calculated that what she spent would have only covered one of Father Ante's shoes. The left one. Was he going to wear them at three o'clock this afternoon, to my parents' wedding? I didn't want that. Part of me hated him for those shoes. But the other part felt sorry for him, because in spite of all our prayers, he still couldn't quit smoking. Sister alone had worried enough for all of us, and yet I didn't feel sorry for her. To me she seemed dumb, and she was strict to the point of being evil, which made me hate her a bit too. But even she had a good side. She couldn't help breaking into a smile when she talked about the archbishop finishing the rectory and buying us a new projector, how if we kept our faith strong, God's mercy would take care of the rest. At those times, an unguarded smile would appear, and her head would gently rock back and forth with quiet pride, like a singer repeating the chorus for the third time. God's mercy didn't fall on the stubby nicotine-stained fingers of a young priest in the suburbs. It didn't and it won't, so better to forget the whole business. In the end, I never understood why we had to pray for him so much, or what the problem with cigarettes was. If it was a question of health, I could understand that, and if sin was the problem, I could understand that too. But I had to separate the two, I couldn't bundle them together. If it was a question of health, and God's mercy was of no help, that meant God doesn't exist. And if it was a sin, and man can't fix sin on his own, God should have intervened, if for no other reason than to spare the thirty of us from having to devote our biweekly prayers to a lost cause. There was also a third possibility. Maybe smoking wasn't a sin worthy of prayer. If that's the case, the whole set-up was wrong, it was all a waste of energy. Prayers in vain.

Friday finally came around. Shortly before three, we parked under the big linden trees next to the church. Pulling up alongside us in their Renault 4 were my aunt and uncle, the witnesses. They were beautifully dressed, as were my parents. Dad, the man in the mask on the other side of the door of room six at the Jordanovac Clinic for Lung Diseases, was wearing a pinstripe navy suit, shiny black shoes, and a gorgeous baby blue tie with a shimmering pink thread. Clean-shaven, with mid-length sideburns and hair parted down the middle, he looked like a foreigner. If he'd started speaking in a different language, I'd have forgotten that I ever had a father who spoke Croatian, worked in a bakery and knew how to use dynamite. Mum's in high heels, wearing a dark skirt and beige shirt, a scarf and summer coat completing her look. Her hair is fixed in place with lots of hairspray. She looks perfect.

As the two of them stand there in front of Father Ante, it occurs to me that right about now, even when he's supposed to be doing a marriage ceremony, he's probably craving a big fat drag. Let him crave. Let God help him, I thought to myself, not without contempt.

My brother and I are standing behind them in our white shirts and belted brown sweaters that Mum knitted. Our thick brown hair is parted to the side and oiled with some of Dad's product, which he'd used to stop our hair from falling on our foreheads. My father, the one now fighting for oxygen in a hospital room. He was such a sweet man, and so proud of his sons.

I had the camera in one of my pockets, the flashbar in the other. Watching the light fall through the clerestory windows, I fumbled about trying to work out whether to use the flash. In the end, I decided that first I'd give it a go without, and that after that I'd put it on and take the rest of the photos with it.

To Father Ante's surprise, I stepped forward and started making my way towards him, my parents about to say those fateful words. Seeing the Kodak, he returned to his duties. I stepped forward and then back, snapping away, the little wheel that winds the film on buzzing like it was supposed to. Then I grabbed the flash from my pocket and took another series of shots. With the afternoon sun streaming in, the church was lit up like an amusement park. By God, you're like a real journo, my uncle whispered. My aunt sighed. Whether *by God* was a swear word, or whether you weren't supposed to talk when someone's getting married, I couldn't tell.

It was all over quickly. Father Ante squeezed their hands and went back behind the altar to the vestry to get changed. The rest of us exchanged kisses, and without making the sign of the cross, walked out, hopped in our cars, and drove off up the hill home. I marvelled at Dad's tie. I couldn't believe I hadn't seen it when I was rummaging through his wardrobe trying on shirts. Just before home, we hit the flat part of the road and saw the *terrebonne* shining in the sun. The side we were facing was all finished. Today they were working on the other side, the high one bordering the sinkhole.

'Christ that Skender's done a good job,' said my father. Although the façade would be paid for with borrowed money, the car swelled with the pride poor people feel when they've outdone themselves. As we pulled up in front of the house, we heard someone yelling, and then Skender rushed past carrying a bloodied Škeljzen in his arms. Blood was pouring from his head and he wasn't showing any signs of life. Mum turned to stone. When Uncle arrived a few moments later, he left the Renault running, just hopped out and shouted:

'Get him in here, put him in the back, we'll take him to emergency.' But Skender was completely lost, his sons staring down from the scaffold like statues, one of them still holding a bucket of *terrebonne*.

'Skender, stop!' Dad bellowed. And Skender stopped.

'Boss, the hospital.'

'How the fuck are we going to do that?' my father demanded.

'Don't ask, boss, don't ask.'

In the meantime, Mum had run inside and brought back a bowl of water and a couple of hand towels. Dabbing the poor kid's head, she revealed the extent of the horror. Beneath his thick head of hair, the wound looked like a burst watermelon.

'Wait, wait,' my father jumped in, loosening his tie so he could breathe.

Skender was already in the backseat of the car, and my uncle had somehow managed to lay Škeljzen back in his arms. Tears streamed down Skender's grief-stricken face. He wasn't the man he was yesterday, not even the one from a few days ago. He wasn't a man, just a knot of raging fear.

'Can I go too, Dad,' I asked, not knowing why.

'C'mon, in the back.'

I sat down next to Skender, our legs touching. He was shaking. Dad floored it. Up front, my uncle pulled a bottle of whiskey from his pocket.

'Sweet fucking Jesus, we couldn't have got there any sooner, could we?'

He offered the bottle to Dad, who took a swig. Skender didn't want any. I didn't even get an offer. I watched Škeljzen's ribcage rise and fall. His head bound in a hand towel, he looked like a little Indian boy in a turban. Sleeping.

'Go fuck yourself, you flaming cow,' my father howled at a woman driver who wouldn't let him change lanes.

'What a bitch,' my uncle chipped in.

'Pass me the bottle a sec, c'mon,' I pleaded.

'Here you go, have a sip,' said my uncle.

Dad wasn't paying any attention. He had it in third, the car roaring its way through the traffic on Marx and Engels Boulevard. I dipped a corner of the towel in the whiskey and spread it around Škeljzen's mouth. Then I dipped it in again and gently dabbed his face. I passed the bottle back, having already accepted the futility of what I'd done. A moment later, Škeljzen stirred, opening his eyes and letting out a groan. He'd regained consciousness and was trying to lift his head up, but his father just held him, beaming, held him close like a pet, his pride and joy.

'It's an emergency, mate, you gotta let us in,' says my uncle.

But the guy on the gate doesn't flinch. So then, in his suit and shiny beige shoes, my uncle gets out of the car and opens the back door. He's gotten hold of Škeljzen and is trying to pull him out of the car.

'For fuck's sake, I'll fucking leave him here on the road and you'll be to fucking blame,' he yells at the guy.

'You can't do that, mate, it's not allowed,' the guy replies, stunned.

In the end, the guy comes out and lifts the barrier with one hand and waves us through with the other, cursing as we drive past. But we couldn't care less. It won't be long before Škeljzen's admitted and seen to, meaning that we'll soon be heading home. Skender won't be back until nightfall. Later, when we're home, my father asks one of our tenants to drive up to the hospital and collect the Albo whose son got all mangled. In his fancy Citroën, the tenant cruises on in, no hassle with the guy at the gate.

'How 'bout you go fuck yourself,' my father says when the tenant tries bragging about it the next morning.

What else happened that evening? We ate, and we drank, and in the end, we sat and watched television – crammed together on the three-seater, sat on wobbly chairs, or spread out on the rug in front of the sideboard. During the day, a few neighbours had come by to offer their congratulations. They'd all sat down with us and ate and drank, but they didn't watch TV. All our best wishes, they'd say, and then start talking about everyday stuff, about work, jobs they were doing around the home, neighbours who were sick or in strife.

I couldn't wait for the morning. It'd be Saturday, but the photo shop down by the stadium would be open. It's not far from here. I'll take the film in to get developed and ask them to put a new one in for me. If the money my parents gave me for the wedding stretches far enough, I'll buy a new flash. But how much does a magic burst of blinding light cost? I didn't care. I wanted a flash. I was shivering with excitement just thinking about tomorrow. When he saw me, my uncle got pretty worried: 'Don't like westerns, huh? They're the best, you'll see.'

The fact is, I actually do like westerns. But my aunt and uncle aren't going anywhere fast, and before long there'll be Turkish coffee on the table and Mum will have emptied two full ashtrays. I decide to shoot to the loo before braving the chill of my room and getting into bed. Outside it's a clear April night. A northeaster blowing, and a full moon. And somewhere nearby, a dog that won't quit howling. My parents had married in the church, meaning that this day will never come again. I know all about the transience of things. I know that every second that vanishes in a second is like a thorn buried in the heart. But I also know that my life has an endless ocean of seconds ahead. Everything has just begun, and yet when I daydream, I rush headlong into the world of grown-ups, longing for what, at least when seen from afar, seems like a miracle. But one thing is clear. A day like today will never come again. You can only get married in the church once. There are exceptions, but they're only granted to important people. That's how sister explained it to us when we were talking about the holy sacraments. I, of course, couldn't help asking how important people managed that. She'd batted the question away with a wave, so I asked why such people got married in the first place, if it's impossible to get married a second time. She cut me off with a 'Don't you upset the other children with your questions.'

'But sister, who are these important people? At least tell me that, if you know.'

'Well, I don't know, so there,' she shot back. For me, my parents are important people. They both suffered hunger as children, sometimes didn't even have bread to eat. Now they've got a house and a car, and they've even got children. That's why they're important people. They walked a long road and they survived. But I've got a feeling that they're not the important people that sister had in mind. In fact, I'm sure of it. That's fine, doesn't matter, I almost whisper. At least my parents won't get divorced and write a letter to the pope asking for permission to get married in the church again. How stupid is that, as if the pope doesn't have better things to do than absolve important people of their poor life choices. They can't expect him to clear a path towards a new sacrament of marriage like a roadworker clearing fallen rocks from the road. That's pretty up yourself, isn't it *Our Father who art in heaven...* I mumbled away, thinking of Father Ante and his cigarettes. To the ferocious howls of the north wind and a lonely dog, I sank into a restless sleep.

Tomorrow, what I'd give for tomorrow to come.

I let the car idle while she buys a small burek pie, yogurt, and some water from the bakery next to our building. Back at home she'd packed an apple and a knife, putting them together in a plastic bag with a banana. For the calcium, she'd said, repeating herself again. We're on our way to the hospital, both of us wound tight. The city is blanketed in smog, only the odd ray of morning sun making it through. The road's jammed, and we sit next to each other in silence as the column in front of us stops and starts. The silence works as a fear generator. One of us needs to say something. But we can't. We listen to the concert programme, and not for the first time, I think how orchestral musicians are truly blessed. And then a split second later, I decide that their lives are a horror show, and that the violin is a kitschy and whiny instrument, and that only dilettantes play the oboe. It's the fear. I need to lug my boulder to the top of this fucking Zagreb hill, all the way to the third floor. Then I need to heave it overhead and smash the doors down, smash them once and for all, deliver us from this silence and dread. But instead, I just say that the music is boring and change the station. 'Turn it off then,' my mother replies. At that moment, our lane starts to flow freely, and through the fog we approach the hospital.

'I wonder how he slept?' my mother ventures.

'Well enough, I reckon. Maybe by now he's gotten used to the hospital a bit.'

'One can only hope.'

'He will have, don't worry. We're doing what we can.'

Relativising things lightens me, helps me ease the heaviness of the drive, but the fear is hard on our trail, pressing at our backs. We arrive at the hospital, already stooped and defeated before we even reach the glass doors where the smokers sneak a cigarette. People with lung tumours, people with no vocal cords, people in wheelchairs with oxygen bottles, the odd high school nursing student, nails long and colourful, waiting to start the day's work experience.

We pass the main reception desk and make our way down the corridor to the lift. The hospital's deserted, except for those in white and the odd downcast civilian. We take the lift to the third floor, the nursing students taking the stairs beside. You can see the kindness in them, irrespective of their age, an age that isn't kind to anyone, years so difficult I wouldn't ever want to go through them again, even in my sleep. The trauma and upheaval, the *Sturm* and *Drang*, no way. On the upside, there's the vitality of a young body, the coiled energy sheathed in skin still smooth and fragrant, eyes without wrinkles, hair, youth. So much beauty, but no way, no way.

'Sit down here and wait. I'm going to find the doctor.'

'Okay,' Mum replies, waiting for the door to open, a half-chance to see Dad. He can't be more than a few metres away, but we're not allowed to visit him. With both of us wearing masks, will he even recognise us?

The office is on this side of the glass door, pretty much in the corridor. But it's locked and there's no one there. A nurse waddles past carrying some kind of folder. She's wearing those funny slip-on shoes with a spring in the sole. She's young, her ears almost dripping with gold. I address one of those ears as if it were a holy relic:

'Excuse me, do you perhaps know when the doctor will be back,' I say, pointing to the office.

'I don't know. What do you need?' the nurse replies.

'We've got something to sort out,' I say in somewhat firmer tone, hoping to avoid further explanation.

'Just wait here, she's not far away. She'll be back soon.'

'Thanks.'

Her earrings quivered as she leaned over, using the card around her neck to unlock the door to the ward. I know Mum will take her chance. She's on edge, the anxiety both tearing her apart and propelling her on.

'Just a moment,' she says to the nurse, but the nurse doesn't hear her.

Mum gets a hand on the door before it closes, heads into the ward, knocks twice on Dad's door, and then, with her bag in hand, steps into the light that is otherwise streaming through the frosted windows. She closes the door and I wait for her to reappear, but she doesn't. She's been in there for ten minutes already. I tell myself it's a good sign. She'll be feeding him, or maybe she's just talking to him. Dad's in there, he's in the room.

Now she's opened the door and is calling me in. I read her lips: there's no one else here. I point at the locked door that leads to Dad's ward. There's a handle on the inside, and she walks over and lets me in. I'm at my father's bedside in a flash. He looks a bit better. Mum thinks it's a good sign that they've reduced his oxygen to 12 litres an hour. 'It is good,' I say, 'it is a good sign.' He removes his mask and asks me when he's going home.

'I can't stay here anymore, I can't. Can't you do something?'

'I am, Dad. You'll be out of here as soon as possible. You're coming home. But it's risky.'

'It's not, it's not,' he tells me. 'It's risky in here, it's worse in here.'

'Go on, go find the doctor,' he says, grabbing my hand, 'go on, Son.'

I kiss him on the forehead and head out into the corridor where a young doctor is marching towards me. Head down, she looks worried. She's carrying a bunch of reports, and stops to read them. Then she frowns, and I sense her fear. There's something she doesn't understand, something that can't be mastered. When I reach Dad's doctor's office, I knock on the door. Absent-minded, my good manners desert me and I go straight for the handle, not expecting it to be open. But it is open, and I almost bust the door down, like a kidnapper. No surprise there, I guess. I'm trying to spring a man out of hospital, spirit him away somewhere he can enjoy some kind of life in the time he has remaining. Audacity is all I've got left.

'Listen,' says the doctor, 'we've got a real problem with discharging him. You said that at home he's got a 12-litre oxygen concentrator?'

'Correct.'

'That's not big enough. He needs access to more litreage, but state health insurance won't approve an additional one for him.'

'Get them to approve a bigger one then. He's a sick man.'

'Of course he is, but there isn't a bigger one, at least not that he can take home. Which is why I recommend a transfer to Knin, where there's a care home for people like him.'

'Knin?'

'Or there's one near Čakovac, but for you down south, Knin's closer.'

'Doctor, I'm begging you. He has to get home, there has to be a way. How about I find another concentrator from somewhere. I'll rent it, join it up with the other one, whatever it takes to get him out of here as soon as possible.'

She nodded silently.

'Okay then, call me tomorrow. Or actually, stop by again around this time. I'm sorry it's like this.'

I sat down by the lift to wait for Mum. We'll go home for a bit. I keep mulling over what I'm going to tell her when I look into her big dark eyes, how I'm going to explain the absurdity with the oxygen concentrator and the litres. But I know that he's too sick to be discharged. The bureaucrats who make the rules and work out the formulas know that too. A man who needs 15 litres of oxygen an hour has to die in hospital. The formula isn't complicated, but fucking with it is my only option. I know my father, and if I succeed in getting him out of here, if I get him home, he'll live a little longer. If I fail, I'll be guilty of having cowered in the face of the storm cloud that has smashed into our chests and is now pressing down on us, insistent, howling at our arrhythmic hearts. Terrorising them.

When Mum turns the doorhandle and starts walking towards me, it feels like I'm in an army muster. I'm being summoned and have to jump to attention and straighten myself up. That same storm cloud, the existential darkness, is calling my name. It's only me now. Only I can do it. I understand this as Mum draws nearer, her eyes becoming ever-expanding black lakes on which a bird of solace has to land, even if it's the smallest bird in the world. A ray of different light on an almost unbearably sunny spring morning.

Before she left, Mum had made us French toast and covered it with a serviette. She'd also poured a jug of orange juice and taken a few bananas from the big pantry. Lunch for me and my brother. Dad's at the bakery. She's at the furniture factory. Yesterday they'd got married in the church and hadn't gone to work. But today, it's a normal Saturday. The workmen are nowhere to be seen. There's just the scaffolding and a few bags of white cement under the tree where they normally sit on concrete blocks and eat from their laps.

They're probably up at the hospital, seeing Škeljzen. Everything's fine. Yet as I told myself that, I went numb, my eyes welling up at the thought of yesterday's rush to the hospital. The feeling of blood on my hands, the smell of Johnny Walker. It was like a movie where they swear like sailors and save someone's young life.

I'm going to head down to get the photos developed. That'll be my morning. Normally you have to wait a few days, but I'm going to try and get them back today, I have to. I put my hand in the dried pumpkin where we keep the bread money and the change for when the neighbours buy stuff. Normally they have the exact amount, but sometimes we just say that they should stop by with the money on their way to work. Other times, you really have to give them their change or strike some kind of deal. I'm taking money from the pumpkin, our cash register, so I can get my film developed. My parents know that I help myself when I need to, and they also know that it's mostly me who fills the pumpkin, that it's me who tears down the stairwell into the garage to get a customer his wine or fill a bottle of slivovitz by sucking it from the barrel with a rubber hose. I'm as shy as can be, but when I take care of this sort of thing, it's like I'm hypnotised. Even when the customers are skunked. That got me thinking – should I take George, who owns the photo shop, a bottle of wine or slivovitz? A kind of bribe to get him to do the film immediately? But he's down there in the city, next to the wide road by the sea where the bus for Trieste goes. He's a man of culture, owns a photo studio, what would he want with our village wine? Skipping the French toast, I stuff the camera in my pocket and head down to the garage. I grab two clean green empties, fill them with wine and jam corks in the top. I take a drawstring bag from the shelf, figuring that I'll be able to put it in my pocket after I've handed over the wine, so it won't annoy me if I want to hang out with friends, or just sit on a bench near the studio and watch the massive crane in the shipyard unloading steel.

I get my stride on, sometimes even breaking into a little trot, but then the bottles of wine on my back start swinging from side to side and I have to slow down. At the bend, at the spot where we slip through a makeshift fence and cut across a muddy excavation site on our way to school, I spotted Skender's truck heading my way. I could see his sons' heads in the cabin, with Skender himself at the wheel, blowing cigarette smoke out the window. Blinded by the glare of the windscreen, I couldn't spot a bandaged head, couldn't even count them, but as far as I could make out, there was no Škeljzen. I waved and they pulled over.

Skender wound the window down and stuck his head out.
'Where ya goin'?'
'I've got something to take care of. How's Škeljzen?'
'Orright, he's gotta rest. Where's ya old man?'
'At the bakery.'
'Righto, we're off to work then. Catch ya later.'

He revved the engine and went to let the handbrake out. At that moment, I decided to ask him where they were from and if they'd ever been to the Sharr Mountains and if they've got any Sharr Mountain dogs. But I was too late. I'd wanted to hear a story along the lines of *White Fang*, but that didn't happen. I stood there in the black cloud of exhaust fumes from their clapped-out old truck.

I lingered for a moment, looking at the photos of men and women in the window display. Couples, wedding portraits. Look at those smiles, the ironed shirts, the immaculate haircuts, the straightened ties. Half an hour later, the bride will be mincing about on the table, the groom and his best man stumbling around, kissing each other's foreheads and howling at the moon. Maybe not though. Maybe there'll be a string quartet and a singer, the guests stabbing silver cutlery into meat served on wide shallow plates before gracefully eating their cake and applauding the young couple. But even here, someone could still cut loose, tear their shirt off, and jump up on the stage. That could happen, couldn't it? What do I know about posh people or sitting up straight at tables with porcelain plates and silver cutlery? As far as these sorts of people go, at least the ones I've imagined, I've always thought there was something ugly about their coldness, a lack of love in their composure. In what kind of home do you have to be born to feel this insecure standing outside a pokey photo studio in a building down the road from a football stadium? In what kind of wilderness did your soul turn from hide to skin, and then from skin into a feeling that you'll never manage to overcome your true nature, to disguise the fact that your father works in a bakery and your mother in a furniture factory, and that no one's ever explained to you how to behave in certain situations? You've learnt these lessons the hard way and you know it all. You can more than hold your own in conversation with adults. You can make small talk with the tenants. It comes naturally to you. It's just, fuck knows, you get a little anxious when you find yourself among strangers who live different lives to your parents. People who earn their living taking pictures, not mixing bread all night or screwing planks of wood together in a haze of sawdust, their face wrapped in an old cloth. Your fear resides in the unsettling realisation that there are people out there who don't suffer the way that your parents have suffered. Once, in front of the school, you stood beside your geography teacher's new Renault Fuego. A magnificent machine, you peered inside, ogled the dials, the luxurious seats with their spacious headrests. The turmoil of knowing what your parents struggled for on a daily basis almost made you sick, the fact that someone else got to sit in a car like this, and got paid to come to school and talk shit with her girlfriends. What was the point of geography, especially for you who knew all the atlases in the school library off by heart. There was no mystery there. You could have taught the subject.

But you never have and never will get in a new Renault Fuego.

I peered through the shop's open door.

There was a man inside, presumably George, the owner, who was standing at the counter sliding photos in little plastic albums. He moved quickly yet deftly, not creasing a single one.

He looked up and said: 'And?'

'Good morning. I've got a film to be developed.'

'Give it here, c'mon.' He'd already grabbed a paper bag and a pen to write the date, format, and any other requests.

'I'm really sorry, but I wanted to ask if I could get them back today. I need the photos today.'

'Matey, you're shitting me.'

'No, seriously, it's important, really important.'

'And why is it so important?'

'Well, sir, the photos are from my parents' wedding, but now they're getting a divorce, so I want to give them the photos, which I took myself, so that maybe they'll stay together.'

George stared at me suspiciously and I knew I had to keep it up, that I couldn't stop now.

'I've brought you some wine.' I put the fishnet bag on the counter, two dark green bottles of red wine gleaming through the holes. 'I'll give you everything I have, if you just do me this favour.'

'C'mon, you really are shitting me,' he replied. But there was a new softness in his voice. Had I pulled it off? I had to keep going.

'Maybe I could give you a hand, tidy the shop, sweep the footpath out front. Whatever you need, I'll do it.'

At that very moment, a woman came in, a gorgeous brunette in a short skirt and what looked like a sportscoat, a white lacy blouse underneath. Her make-up was caked on and she had a little handbag wrapped around her wrist. She said hello as if I wasn't even there and told George that she needed a passport photo.

'Not a problem, take a seat over here,' he said, pointing to a stool with a big lever to adjust the height.

He looked at me almost flustered. 'I'll sort it. Now take a walk,' he said, shooing me away.

'Would it be possible to take a few portrait shots for the display window?' George asked. 'In that case, I obviously wouldn't charge for the passport photos. They're neither here nor there.'

I left, sat down on the low stone wall, and looked out to sea. My father had learned to swim in a dip in a field which would turn into a little lake after heavy winter rain. As the summer approached, and before the water dried up completely, they'd go swimming there. My mother was born in a village by the sea. She'd learned to swim at the age of four when her much older brother pushed her off a rock and watched her sink until she eventually managed to stay afloat, choking on her tears. I didn't learn to swim until I was seven, at a camping ground where the sea was really dirty and people stood around smoking and chatting in knee-deep water. For a good two years I pretended to do freestyle, lingering in the shallows, my outstretched fingers touching the bottom.

It was there in the crowd that I hid my inadequacy, and it was there that I somehow triumphed over my fears. A few years before, sharks had been spotted off this stretch of coastline. They'd followed the fishing boats in. People said that the fishermen had been throwing fish guts over the side, letting blood flow into the water. I had no idea about the type of fish or how much guts we were taking about. But as my arms searched for the sea floor, every tiny wave felt like a shark's fin brushing by. If my arms couldn't reach the bottom, I was already in the deep, the dangerous deep.

I heard footsteps behind me. The woman was finished in the shop and I could go back. Inside, George was changing the lens on a camera as if under some kind of spell.

'What did we agree then?'

'Well, um.'

'You need your photos quick smart, right?'

'Yes, that's right.'

I noticed that the bottles of wine weren't there on the counter anymore. I better ask him about the fishnet bag, otherwise Mum will wonder where it went.

'Okay then, we're not too busy. Come back just before one.'

I put the film on the glass vitrine and swallowed my question about the bag.

He snatched up the film and smiled.

I checked my watch. It was just after ten. I'll head down to the harbour beside the stadium and watch the barges, hang about close by. I thought about all the free time I had and how that made me a free man. Unlike George, let's say, who'd be off to a wedding tonight, a first communion tomorrow, and then a funeral the day after in a never-ending loop. But I can't say a word against him. No way. To get what I wanted, I'd lied to him. Walking there alongside the rusty spikes of the stadium's perimeter fence, a shiver ran down my spine just thinking about it. My obsession with getting those photos meant that, in a single sentence, I'd managed to divorce my parents, who'd only just got married before God. But God won't care, and neither will they. They're perfect for each other, my lie is harmless. And it's up to Father Ante to sort God out. Though our meetings are less and less frequent, he still takes my confession. When I enter that dark, brown booth with its wooden bars, and I hear him breathing on the other side, when I smell that cigarette stink, I know I have to talk about the kind of stuff that I don't want to talk about to anyone. And the more often I skip confession, the deeper he probes when I am there, right down to the ugliest details. So I leave confession in despair, drenched in sweat, bathed in lies cooked up on the spot. He always wanted to know way too much about my sins, about the stirrings of a young man in the body of a boy. Behind his closed eyes, he wanted to watch the extended cut of a very private film. I quickly worked out that the absolution of sin didn't require you to ask or know very much. You just needed to be repentant, sincerely repentant. But I was unrepentant, sincerity didn't come into it. I knew the torture would soon be over, that this dark booth and its bars, the whole thing stinking like an ashtray, would soon be empty, and that I'd be out of there.

'Hello, yes, that's me. That's great, thank you, of course, that's great news.'

'What's going on? Is that the doctor,' my mother asks before I've even hung up.

'It was. They're going to discharge him tomorrow. He's going home.'

'Mother of God, thank you, thank you,' she said, staring at me, her big eyes full of fear.

At the harbour there's just the odd cat and a pensioner or two. The sun dances in the mooring ropes, the wind sending ripples across the calm surface of the green water. I sit on the stone wall and watch the cats, tails held high, tiptoeing the length of the breakwater. Fur glistening, masters of the port. Two old seadogs are sanding something on a barge, *Vagabond* painted on the starboard side. I'll wander over, see what they're doing. Boredom was seldom so sweet. Right about now, my photos would be soaking in some kind of solution, shimmering there in the darkroom. In the red lamplight, George's indifferent face would now be looking at the faces in my photos. At my parents, at the wedding. What had I achieved? Were they any good? My doubts plagued me as time dragged on. I stood there next to the *Vagabond*, which had started rocking as the two of them pottered about inside. I could make out the sound of a hand sander, and then spotted an extension cord plugged into a power box on the breakwater. I thought of Mum and the machine she operated, the gigantic piece of heavy machinery onto which I'd sometimes help her lift wooden panels. And I thought about physical labour as a lifelong affliction. If you get used to it as a child, you'll never, ever, get rid of it. You'll always be an ox and work with your body. You'll never be a George, Nikon slung over your right shoulder, little accessory bag for film and lenses, strutting about, snapping away, making the magic sound a camera makes.

I head back up thinking they might be done. I make a quick ascent of the slope next to the stadium, jog across the wide road, and then practically fly those last fifty steps to the studio.

'Hello again.'

'Here you go, all done,' said George, handing me an envelope full of photos.

'This one here's on the house,' he said as he grabbed a plastic frame and slipped a photo that was bigger than all the others inside it. It was my parents and my aunt and uncle, plus my brother, who happened to have raised his arm outside the frame of the shot. The milky afternoon light streamed through the church doors behind them. They stood there up at the front, radiant and immortal. In my photo.

I got out all the money I had on me and placed it on the counter. 'Will that cover it?' I asked George.

He put it in the drawer without counting it. 'Bang on,' he said.

'Will it stretch to a flash like this one?' I took a burnt-out flashbar from my pocket.

'Nope, and I don't have one like that anyway. You'd have to go to Italy or somewhere.'

'Can you put a new film in for me?'

'Sure.'

He was done in a few seconds. Then he headed for the door and took his coat from the hanger. It looked like he was closing up.

'Thanks,' I said. 'And could I please have the fishnet bag that I brought the wine in back?'

'What bag?'

'That one there.'

'Now you're definitely shitting me,' he replied, a quiet smile on his face. He went out the back and tossed the bag on the counter to me. I tore off to a bench that was shaded by an overhanging tree. I could finally sit down and look at my photos in peace and quiet, to see how I'd captured the world for the first time, an event that by all accounts would never happen again. I was happy with my work.

'I'll go alone. They won't let you in anyway,' I tell my mother. We're going home to the village tomorrow. While Mum and Dad are in the ambulance with the big bottle of oxygen, I'll set off in the car a few hours ahead, so I can be there to meet the guy from Zadar who has to hook up the other concentrator. I've paid the rental in advance. Four hundred Croatian kuna a month for 360 litres of oxygen, which the concentrator will pump into a little tube that runs the length of the hallway, then across the ceramic tiles in the kitchen, and then on into the living room to the three-seater where my father will be. That's his end-station. I know that, but after all the angst with the hospital, our living room is a kind of Arcadia where he'll be able to spend a little more borrowed time.

My hands are sweaty. I've never done anything this risky. I'd signed the discharge papers at the hospital, taking full responsibility. Now it's up to me. In my hands are all the fragile, precious things that were previously beyond my control. If I lose them now, who knows what will happen. I didn't have a choice. That's what I tell myself. Preoccupied, I push my hair up off my forehead and scratch my scalp like a chimpanzee, mannerisms that are completely new to me. It's the fear at work, inscribing itself on a body that is half a century old, yet now somehow strange.

'But you know I have to come along,' my mother says.

'I know, but you're not allowed inside because of the pandemic. You know that.'

'You say I'm not allowed, but I don't have any choice, so that means I am allowed. I'll just go a couple of metres down the corridor, no one will even see me.'

And she's right, of course, she can't help it. I'm just embarrassed because of our doctor, because I've begged her to do something you can't usually beg for. 'What if she sees us sneaking around,' I ask my mother.

'Who cares if she sees us, we're only human. She knows that.'

'It's pretty awkward,' I tell her.

'Imagine how awkward it is for him, Son. You've seen him, pricked to pieces, his hands all blue. It's harder for him.'

My mother's right. And my hesitation about her going up to see Dad has got nothing to do with getting a dirty look from a doctor. The problem is my weakness. I'd handle all this better alone, that's how it should be. I can cope with whatever, just as long as I don't have to see my mother having to bear more than she can handle. For the first time, she's truly scared, and can't see a way out.

'We haven't had enough time to come to terms with certain things.' That's what she'd told me in the car yesterday on the way home from the hospital.

'There's nothing else we can do,' I replied.

'There isn't, but that doesn't make it any easier.'

We need to look at it as a tiny triumph. We're getting him out of hospital, and he's coming home. That's the best that can happen now. I keep repeating this simple formula, one that doesn't factor in the travel risk or what the trip might take out of him. In his depleted state, all the oxygen machines in the world can't stop him from running out of breath and shutting down for a few minutes, losing the colour in his face and disappearing from the world around him. Only when he finds a tiny pocket of air do his lungs slowly splutter back to life, his eyes clear, and the colour return to his cheeks. Standing at his bedside, holding his hand, Mum and I had silently endured so many of these moments of terror. The waiting for air.

At the hospital drop-off zone, a guy in a white Mercedes with Osijek plates was abusing the guy operating the gate. 'Lift the fucking barrier fuckhead,' says the man, his curses ricocheting off the rosary beads dangling from his rear-view mirror. He revs his rumbling diesel engine until it belches a cloud of black smoke which engulfs Mum and me as we make our way towards the entrance. The gate operator shuts the window of his booth in fear, gesturing that he can't lift the barrier arm, that only hospital vehicles are allowed in.

As we enter the building, I glance over my shoulder and see the Mercedes reversing away from the entrance, the tyres squealing. This cheers me, but the victory is short-lived. When we leave the building half an hour later and pass those smoking and drinking Pelinkovac, the meathead in the Mercedes is parked outside the main doors, blocking the ramp where the bedridden and wheelchair-bound come in and out. And no one can do a damn thing.

We hurry to the third floor. Standing there in the reception area with a colleague was the doctor who'd told me that flour is more damaging to your lungs than tobacco smoke. All Dalmatian cool, he's a bit of a poser; charming, yet somehow bored and detached. I mean, what else can a specialist do in a hospital other than bore himself stupid.

'Hi, doctor, how are things?'

'Oh, I didn't see you there,' he replied, a look of near mischief on his face.

My mother headed straight over to sit down on a bench against the wall, next to the crater for the new lift.

'How's your father doing?'

'Pretty bad. But he's off home tomorrow.'

'You're doing the right thing,' he said approvingly, 'hospitals are pretty messed up places.' Then he laughed. Cynically, of course, but with a hint of sadness in his voice. I didn't doubt that he meant well. It's just that he's an arrogant prick. He can't help it. On the other hand, while he was talking to me, I was almost certain that he'd wanted to offer some kind of reassurance.

'Try not to worry. You've taken incredible care of him. It'll go as well as it can,' he declared from on high.

'Thanks, doctor. And so you know, I've been thinking about what you said about the flour.'

'Yeah?'

'Whether it's really possible that flour could do that much damage to your lungs.'

'Definitely,' he replied, 'definitely.'

With that, he offered me his hand and said goodbye.

I remained stranded there in the middle of the waiting area. It was as if someone was pouring a finely-ground flour over me, covering me with it, the sprinkling sound a gentle whisper. As if I was surrendering to a state of grace, surrendering to death, as if I didn't care anymore and had given up and was now simply letting things happen, because I'm powerless to control them. Yet as the mountain of flour reaches the ceiling, and the waiting area becomes a total whiteout, I realise that I want to fight. Breathless, I snap out of my funk and head over to press the buzzer. 'How can I help,' a voice replies through the speaker. I lower my mouth to the microphone, and with an awkward attempt at charm, mumble Azecolab... and the door opens. I call Mum over and in a split second we're in room six. Both beds are empty.

Mum lets out a cry.

'Wait, wait,' I say, 'sit down.' She crumples down into the chair next to the bed and buries her face in her hands. I go and knock on the door of the room where the nurses are. Not waiting for a reply, I charge in.

'I'm sorry, where's my father?'

'You're not supposed to be here,' a nurse replies.

'I know.'

'We transferred him to room nine.'

Something heavy fell from me. Death's leaden harness. I heard it rattling at the nurse's feet next to the damp mop the cleaner had just used to disinfect the floor.

'But you can't go there, sir.'

'I know, I know.'

Now I was the nicest, the sweetest and most humble man in the world. I was an angel begging to be mounted on a gable, to remain among the living so I could bear witness to their transience.

'But I'm begging you. Two minutes.'

'Go on, be quick,' the young woman softened.

I went back to Dad's old room where Mum was on her feet, staring at the wall.

'He's in room nine.'

'Oh my Lord, thank you,' she sobbed.

We rushed down the corridor, knocked, and let ourselves into room nine. He lay there right beside the door, alone. His eyes shone when he saw us, and when Mum sat down and took out some food, he even managed to get himself up onto his side and lean on his elbow, totally calm and collected. It was the most important moment of his short stay in hospital, one all three of us shyly and silently celebrated.

Mum glanced at the dial where the oxygen tube came out of the wall. It was set to nine litres. 'Gosh, that's amazing how much things have improved,' she said.

She quickly gave him something to eat, and I told him that he was going home tomorrow.

'I know,' he replied. 'I haven't forgotten. I know.'

'You take the tram home. I have to go down to the second floor and see the doctor, sort out all the details. Who knows how long it'll take.'

'It's fine, I'll wait. I'll sit outside on a bench.'

'But it's cold.'

'No, it's not.'

'Come off it, Mum.'

'It's not. Have you sorted everything out with the guy from Zadar?'

'I have.'

'And you know where the house key is?'

'Yep. It's under the houseleek on the balustrade, under the vase.'

'It's not under the vase, it's in the vase. But I don't think I even locked up.'

'Don't worry about it now. Let's go back to the apartment. We've got all day to sort it out.'

'Just so you know, I'm coming back up to see him this afternoon.'

'No, c'mon. It's a shambles up here.'

'No one even saw me. They only saw you.'

'Okay, fine. I'll drive you.'

I walk up the hill, the framed picture of my parents' wedding against my chest so it doesn't break. The rest of the photos are in the fishnet bag slung over my shoulder. I've made sure that the people in the photos are all facing my body. They're private, I say to myself defiantly, huffing and puffing my way up the slope. They're mine, they're my family. I love them, and now I've stolen them from oblivion. Sure, some of the photos are duds, but a few are really special. I don't care if someone is missing an arm or a leg or half their face, or if someone's got red eyes because of the flash. Ever since I was little, I've had my own sense of what constitutes beauty. The photos are no exception.

The photo I'm holding now is from the pile Mum brought with her on the trip to Zagreb, to the hospital. 'How strange,' she'd said, 'I only grabbed a few photos to have them with me.' I don't know when we'd last looked at them, when she'd last looked at them. Death was drawing near. That's the only way I can explain what can't be explained. Now she's there in the room next to mine, reading a book. Glasses on the tip of her nose, she reads a couple of pages and then puts it down and sobs. Sometimes, when I walk down the hallway, I hear a choked whimper. But on this journey, there's no one who can help her, him, or me. There are no shortcuts, no cosy lay-bys, or quiet oases; no hitchhikers whose blabbering might gradually open the curtains that are closing on the days that remain. There's no respite, time doesn't fly, it just slows, and in the end, everything dissolves. Tomorrow we'll be on the motorway. I'll head off a few hours before them and get everything ready, open the blue metal gate to the yard, as if a wedding party might accidentally come our way. In the house, those beautiful machines will already be humming away, their long life-giving tubes at the ready.

Dad came into my room, still wearing the shirt in which he'd come home from the bakery.

'Wanna go for a ride to pick the young fella up?'

Skender was already waiting in the car. Sitting there in his overalls, he hadn't had time to get changed. Mum had asked one of our neighbours who was an orthopaedic nurse at the hospital to keep an eye on "the little Albo." She'd come by a little while ago and said that it was okay to go and get him, that the doctor had given the go-ahead. His brothers downed their buckets, trowels, and the hoes they used to mix the *terrebonne*, before quickly scrubbing their hands and faces.

'The boys'll stay here, but they won't be working, they'll just wait,' Skender explained. 'You don't work without the boss, gotta watch the quality,' he said with pride and conviction.

I sat in the back. Our old car was a column shift, and Dad, getting into the rally spirit, dropped the gears and set us off down the hill in second. There on the backseat, I stuck my head between the two men so I could better see the road curve ahead of us and watch the traffic lights turn green. When Dad floored it at a set of lights on the main boulevard, squealing tyres and all, Skender turned to him and said: 'appreciated, boss.'

I was expecting an argument at the gate, but we just cruised on through, the barrier already up. We parked outside the ward and bounded up to Škeljzen's floor. Dressed in my pants and tracksuit top, he was sitting there waiting in his room. Unbeknown to us, Mum had asked the neighbour to bring him some clothes. 'Mums know,' that's all she'd said when Dad asked her about it later. 'It was a lovely thought,' he said. 'Poor kid, all on his own here. No mother, not even a sister.'

Škeljzen, the youngest son, got up out of bed as soon as he saw us, his father giving him a hug.

'Heya Škeljzen,' I said.

'Heya, how's it?' he replied.

My father knocked on the reception desk in the corridor and told the nurse that we're going to take the little fella home now.

'Is there anything we have to sign?'

'Everything's there in his room,' the nurse replies, painting her nails.

On a saucer behind her are two empty cups of coffee turned upside down. Am I going to get married and be rich? the cups ask. Married yes, rich no, a young larrikin chips in as he strolls past with three other men, the youngest of whom has a bandaged head.

He can sleep at our place until you're done, my mother tells Skender.

'No need, Ma'am.'

'For Christ's sake, what's the problem. We've got room!' my father bellows.

Škeljzen sat in silence, scoffing the Neapolitan wafers Mum had put out. They were all having coffee. On the table there's a huge cezve on whose walls destiny itself is written, markings to while away the hours. If only the nurse at the orthopaedic reception could see this kind of luxury.

'He can share our son's room. We've got the space, honestly. You'll be finished in a day or so. Let the boy rest up.'

'It's very kind, Ma'am, I'll never forget this. You're good people, a good family,' Skender says, turning to my father and offering him his hand. I thought they were saying their goodbyes, but then I worked out that it was actually a sign of affection and respect. They hung about sipping their coffee and smoking, chatting about the façade. No one mentioned Škeljzen again.

*

Mum got a mattress and put it down in the middle of my room, making up a bed with a sheet and a pillow. Then she told me to strip my bed and put clean sheets on it for Škeljzen. I'd be on the floor, if that was okay with me, she asked.

'Course, why wouldn't it be.'

Maybe I should show her the photos now, I thought.

'Mum, look.' I opened the sideboard and took out the framed picture from their wedding. She was gobsmacked.

'Good God, where'd you get that?'

'I made it. I mean, it's one of my photos.'

'But when did you get it developed and framed?'

'On Saturday.'

'And you've kept quiet about it until now? Oh my big boy!' She hugged me, and then brought her hands, calloused and rough from the sanders, to my chubby cheeks.

'Thank you, Son, you are the sweetest, sweetest boy. I can't believe it. There we all are.' She called out to my father: 'Come here, c'mon, look at this!'

And he came in and said that he'd bang a nail in the living room wall and hang it up straightaway. 'Bravo, Son, Get the hammer and a nail, in the garage.'

Škeljzen only spent a couple of nights in my room. During the day he does a bit of work with his father and brothers, carrying half-full buckets of *terrebonne*. His brothers often tell him to go and lie down. The white turban on his head soon turns grey from the cement dust, the stitched wound slowly closing, healing over, and disappearing beneath his woolly brown hair. This sad reminder of the fall fades into the darkness of oblivion and slowly disappears.

We spend both nights whispering in the lamplight. Flicking through the pages of a huge atlas of the world, we barely understand each other. Škeljzen is obsessed with photos of tropical beaches, completely mesmerised. I practically interrogate him about his village, his house, his family, even about his dogs, those famous Sharr Mountain dogs. His Croatian was pretty bad, but I managed to pick up that an uncle of his likes to go hunting, and that another uncle had fallen down a ravine and died while out hunting bears, just like Škeljzen fell off the scaffold. 'Same shit,' he said, 'y'know.'

The scaffolding is down, the house glistening in white. The truck's loaded, the sons already in the cabin. I gave my new friend a hug and he invited me to come and stay with him, in the winter, when they're not working: 'Come down, stay as long as you want. Dad said that you have to be our guest.'

'Thanks, Škeljzen, thanks.'

At the table, my father is counting German marks, Skender sipping his coffee. Mum's baked a marble cake and wrapped it in tinfoil, for the trip, she says.

When Dad's finished counting, he picks the money up from the glass table and hands it to Skender.

'Here you go, skipper, you did a great job.'

'Pleasure,' Skender replies, and takes three hundred-mark notes from the top of the pile. 'That's a discount.'

'No need, you'd do the same. It's what people do,' says my father.

'C'mon, mate, please.'

'Alright,' says Dad.

'And one more thing. If you're ever down our way, give us a shout. We'd love to have you, love to show you around.'

'That's very kind, skip. Very kind.'

Skender stood up, offered Mum and Dad his hand, and headed for the door. Then he turned around and took a step back towards me. Offering me his hand, he bent down a little and said: 'See ya, matey.'

Aunty and Uncle came over that same night, and our tenants came up the stairs. Our living room was full of people sitting around drinking and raising toasts. Dad got out the prosciutto that Grandad had sent by bus from the village. I organised the wine, and Mum poured it into the big grey glasses with the wicker holders at the base. The glasses will end up at the house in the village where we're taking my father tomorrow, where my parents have been living for the past fifteen years. Where the family tomb is.

There's lots of animated conversation and throaty laughter. Our house is like a ferry sailing on a balmy spring night. A glistening white cacophony of joyous noise. For tonight, we've pushed the table up against the wall. Hanging there above it on a special concrete nail is the photo I took of my parents, the one George framed for me for free. The era of raw brick was gone, the stigma of us having no money. The red unrendered house had disappeared from our street forever, yet the shame of poverty lived on. That's a crossing you can't make overnight.

I'm looking at that exact same photo tonight, just in a smaller format, agonising over whether I should be driving my seriously ill father home in order to honour his last wish. Or at least one of his last. The weaker Dad got, and the quieter and more incomprehensible his speech – muffled by both the mask and the hissing of the oxygen tubes – the more intensely I listened to him, absorbing his words in advance. There was never any hiding from any of this. No refuge, no sanctuary. Just constant exposure to the wound. On the way to the hospital, sometimes I had the feeling that at every set of lights, someone was going to jump in the car and mug us, suffocate us, and then suddenly let us go. And just as we got our breath back, as the life returned to our bodies, the whole ordeal would start again. Sitting in the waiting room next to the hole in the wall for the lift, surrounded by workmen and their thunderous drilling, the sense of suffocation returned. As the dust rose from the drilling, the only thing I could see was flour, pernicious and malignant, getting down into our lungs, accumulating there.

Tomorrow we hit the road, however things turn out, whatever happens. I wanted someone to whisper that to me, to reassure me, but there was no one to perform that role, no one who had the strength. I am the eldest son, I live in Zagreb, and I'm standing on a precipice from which at any moment I could tumble down into the deepest ravine. I am responsible for everything: for hope, for humour, for food and water, for conditions on the road, for the bottle of oxygen that has to last the whole trip, for the doctor who made an exception, for the guy who's coming from Zadar with the extra concentrator, for everyone in the village wondering about their neighbour, even for the electricity needed to keep the concentrators humming, which also makes me responsible for thunder and lightning, not to mention any work needed on the powerlines. For all the pain and the gasping for air in the chest and lungs, I am responsible. And as I stand on one leg atop that steep granite ridge, holding a photo of a distant wedding where the light's at my parents' backs, it's only now I see that those were days of white, of light. The *terrebonne* and the crushed glass, the afternoon, my mother's blouse, everything. That day we all wore white shirts to the church. Father Ante's fingers are the only yellow, God save him. He's the type of person who sneaks a smoke in front of the oncology ward. But he carries the burden of our prayers, the matters of our pure hearts. He bears the weight of my confessions, the darkness and unease I feel each time the confessional door closes behind me and I head to the altar to pray for forgiveness. But I never actually prayed. I'd just kneel there and try to banish the despair that made my head hurt and my stomach churn. I'd yet to discover the kind of rage that could save your life, the kind of profanity that can make it all better. Go fuck yourself, you fucking cow, that's what my father had yelled at the woman who wouldn't let him change lanes on Marx and Engels Boulevard when he was driving Škeljzen to the hospital. I saw it as a kind of deliverance. The day will come when with a pit in my stomach, I'll kneel down and instead of a prayer, I'll do it, I'll say – go fuck yourself.

And at that moment, the organ and its finely-wrought pipes will swell. The flutes of God.

III

I HAVEN'T slept well. It's more like I've swallowed it in small flavourless portions, the way a busy waiter eats during a shift. I wake constantly with my heart pounding, and at these times I inhale deep into my chest and try to steady things. But it doesn't help. At certain moments it seems like I'm entirely at the whim of whatever awaits me, and that I don't stand a chance of pulling it all off. We're dependent on so many things – people we've never met, conditions on the road, and not least, how Dad, the passenger, feels when he wakes up. The uncertainty is like a gong resounding in my heart, its metallic sound travelling out into the emptiness until it hits the external wall and surges back in a kind of spasm, crashing up into my throat. I keep having to go to the kitchen for a drink. Mum's in the living room. Is she asleep?

Her face is turned towards the window, the silence of the night stealing through the narrow gaps in the blinds. It's early spring, the start of a new week, the city at rest.

The local hoods aren't quite ready for their motorbikes, still driving their drugs and their barbie dolls around in cars. Soon enough they'll be hooning up and down the flat stretch between the two traffic lights, right under my balcony, rearing up on their back wheels, frightening pedestrians and the passengers in passing trams.

Around four in the morning, someone starts running a bath, the jet hitting the enamel and then the water. The drone goes on forever. Someone's about to ease in there, light up a cigarette, and have a good old soak in the foam.

God the fearful are moody bastards!

As afraid as I am, I can't see an alternate route, just the one I've chosen. Today's mission is perilous, and there's no margin for error.

Because oxygen is running out.

I take an apple and pick up the pile of photos. Maybe the life that unfurls from them will help bring calm to life here tonight: memories of life's beauty, moments of grace to balance out the heaviness, or perhaps just some kind of equilibrium that'll let me sleep, at least for an hour, before the morning's rally.

I'm sitting at a wedding with my father and my late uncle. A cousin is getting married. I'm seventeen years old and remember it well because that same year my aunt got a granddaughter. My cousin is pregnant, but we don't know that.

It's a small wedding, a backyard affair for about thirty. The patio doors are flung open and there's a constant stream of neighbours and random passers-by. Two of the guests are arm in arm in song, *sing to me, my hawk, sing to me*. I'm sitting on a chair next to their table and someone has just taken a photo. That's the photo I'm holding now. It's the only time I've heard my father sing, and I'm stunned by his deep, rich voice. Yet it's as if he's holding back somehow, lagging behind, hesitating. He's got his arm around a guy who's been dead for years, the coal-haired husband of my mother's sister. I'm sitting there in a navy jumper with a sprig of rosemary pinned to my chest, brown dress trousers, and calf-high leather boots with big heels and a gold band around the ankle. I've only just bought them. I'd wanted to get real cowboy boots, and had saved up the money I'd earned from reading gas meters. Try as I might, I just couldn't get them up over my calves, and even if I'd managed, my jeans wouldn't have made it back down. I had thick brown hair brushed over to one side, the hair at the back falling a few centimetres over my collar. My hair would often flop down over my right eye, and I'd flick it back up with my hand. It was all the rage at the time, and I cared about stuff like that. I'd just started shaving, and every few days I'd remove the bum fluff from my chin and upper lip. I had dark eyebrows, full lips, and clear skin, not a pimple in sight. Although I was happy with the way I looked, my legs were a source of both pride and grief. I was pretty solid from playing competitive handball for years, and you could make out my shoulders under my jersey and my rock-hard thighs under my pants. I'd sat down to try and ward off the tedium of the wedding. There was a record playing, and most people were chatting, singing, and eating. But no one was dancing, and no one offered a toast. Not the parents, not the relatives who'd travelled up from their villages, not even one of the bride and groom's young friends. They were first-generation urban dwellers, normal working people, and didn't know any better. Just happy-go-lucky folk enjoying an open-door November wedding as the northeaster drove bone-cutting rain into the night.

My father's wearing the same tie he wore to his wedding, its pink thread shimmering in this photo too. My uncle is laughing, but my father looks serious. I remember him that night, and not just because I heard him sing. At around two in the morning, one of the younger guests started singing a song I'd never heard before. Something about the Ustasha and our man in Madrid. 'Who's our man in Madrid?' I'd asked, surprised to hear the name of a foreign city at a wedding in Yugoslav suburbia.

'Who's our man in Madrid,' I repeated. This time my father answered: 'Pavelić. Stay clear of those muppets. They'll get us all locked up.'

'I'll go talk to them,' I replied, heading towards a cuddled-up pair. They were drunk, and when they spotted me in the middle of the room, they waved me over, figuring I'd come to join them. The girl, a year or so older than me, kissed me on the cheek and dragged me by my jumper until I was wedged between her and her beanpole boyfriend. I'd never seen them before, never heard the song. I wriggled free and got up on tip-toes to tell the boyfriend's ear to quit it. He placed the five bony fingers of his enormous palm on my head and gently pushed me away. He might have said something if he hadn't been so wasted, but he didn't. I left the room, shut the door to the hallway and went out onto the balcony. It didn't make any difference. You could still hear everything. I stood out there in the cold, looking down the street thinking that the cops would be here any minute to shut it all down. What a circus. What the hell's wrong with these people? In a moment, my father will come out to tell me that things are getting out of hand and that we'd be on our way soon. I remember us silently walking the three hundred metres home, the northeaster blasting the potholes dry. About halfway, at a spot where you could see the bay, I gazed down into the darkness below, out to the distant lights of the little town on the island across the water. The townspeople were enjoying the kind of peaceful sleep you read about in fairy tales, the kind of sleep that existed before mass slaughter was invented. This absence of fear was quite a contrast to the historical atlas I almost knew off by heart. It told only of war, and no one, not a single one of the six and a half billion people on earth, seemed innocent. Not even the four of us. Not my mother or my sleepy brother, who she was leading by the hand, and not me or father, the two of us walking side by side.

I'm burlier and taller, and not only because of my boot heels.

Should I tell him now, tell him what I did yesterday before practice, on the way home from school? We'd never walked anywhere together at night, never been for a walk full-stop. If I don't find the courage to get it off my chest now, I don't think I ever will.

And it's important to me that I do.

Because I might have killed someone.

But instead of coming out with it, I stall. I don't care that the weight is crushing me or that my knuckles are still swollen. I'm not breathing a word, not telling a soul. The knuckles will settle. I took my hands out of my pockets and threw an arm around my father, which is how we walked all the way to our unlocked house. We weren't afraid of anyone.

The bus station had been pretty crowded. I was on my way to handball practice, which didn't start until eight. The station was next to the marina, and having a bit of time, I'd taken the Corso, praying that there'd be enough room for me to put my blue Adidas bag down on the ground. I didn't mind standing, but the bag, stuffed with school books and training gear, was a pain. It's cold, and town's busy. I watch the flow of lights streaming westwards. Long bendy busses come and go, but the number one is nowhere in sight. I turn my collar up against the wind and place my bag at my feet, trying to avoid the gobs of spit on the asphalt. The northeaster has come to life, holding the clamour of the night in its clutches, ripping through the huddled masses, who, like me, have nowhere to hide. The width of the footpath separates two buildings, one a boutique that sells imported jeans and is owned by a wealthy hairdresser and her son. The son does laps out front of my school in a souped-up red Fiat convertible, a gold watch and bracelet on his wrist, the buttons on his pink polo shirt undone, so everyone gets a good look at his thick gold chain. Sitting opposite the station is the Borovo department store where I once bought some Puma trainers, *handball* imprinted in gold lacquer on the leather trim. It didn't matter that they were probably knock-offs, I strutted to practice in them. The next day a bunch of my friends rushed out to get a pair, but they were all gone and the store never had them again. I checked out people's sneakers at every game and at every tournament, but I never saw anyone else wearing them. I loved shoes, that much I can admit. I'd wanted cowboy boots, but with all the exercise, my anatomy refused.

It was freezing, and a crowd of people had now gathered, all waiting for the same bus as me. I buried my hands in the pockets of my peacoat. My uncle's company paid a tailor to make coats for its workers, with the right to a new one every three years. But my uncle preferred the puffy snow jacket he'd bought in Trieste to this elegant one, which was navy, double-breasted, and had a double row of gold buttons with anchors stamped on them. Last month he'd taken me to get measured up. Wearing a custom-made coat eased the pain of not being able to wear cowboy boots, at least to some extent.

As the number seven came in, people jostled and almost trampled each other. I moved aside and ended up next to a guy who was staring at me with an inscrutable smile. I looked the other way and put my bag back down, having picked it up just before the stampede. The guy came over and pressed himself up against me from behind, before slowly inching back. Even with the wind, I could still feel his breath on me, so I shuffled forward. He followed and again bumped himself up against me. I spun around, thinking someone must have pushed him. But no, he was just standing there smirking, his eyes ablaze. For a moment I thought I knew him and that it was all some kind of joke. He was about fifty. Leather jacket, black velvet trousers, polished pointy shoes with thin laces.

He gave me the creeps. I picked my bag up and walked to the far end of the station, not really knowing why. Soon enough he was back at it, pushing himself up against me from behind. This time he spoke.

'C'mon. I'll buy you dinner at a hotel.'

'No, no thanks,' I stuttered.

In that instant, I finally understood at least something of his intentions. And again, I picked up my bag and moved away, leaving him there grinning. At the bottom of the street, I spotted the packed number one bus at the light, spluttering its way towards the station. The whole episode would be over in about ten seconds. Together with my fellow passengers, I'd soon be tumbling my way westwards, to the sports hall and its weights and resin-soaked handballs.

A modest stream of people trickled out the front exit, while the river of us who'd been waiting poured in through the double doors in the middle. I was there in the current, waiting to be swept inside.

I looked over my shoulder. The maniac was nowhere in sight.

When I finally made it in the door, for a good second or two I felt a hand squeeze my buttock and another hand squeeze my genitals. Even in the crowd, I felt the same breath on my neck, between my hair and my collar. I twisted around and bulldozed those behind me. The guy was standing there on the footpath just a couple of metres away.

Still with that shit-eating grin.

I launched myself at him, hurling him a few metres in the air until he fell backwards onto a heap of stacked boxes they'd only just taken out of the boutique. Throwing my bag aside, I got on top of him and started punching him as hard as I could. He was soon lying lifeless under me, his blood running down the Italian flags on the boxes. The sea of people around us had receded, and it was only then that I realised what I'd done. I sprung to my feet, sorted myself out, and grabbed my bag. What now?

Unrepentant and totally aware of what I was doing, I went over and gave the guy a few good kicks.

I then slipped off between the buildings, into the darkness of the old town's narrow streets, trying to get myself under control. Under a flickering street light, I took my towel out and wiped my hands, the blood having already cooled and dried in the howling wind. If I killed him, at least a hundred people saw me. The police won't have any trouble finding me. If I didn't kill him, then who cares. The shame is yet to arrive, and the only thing I feel right now is blind rage and the overwhelming urge to give someone else a hiding. I haven't fired all my shots. But I'm cold, and I'm a mess. And then I realise that my coat only has two of its eight gold anchor buttons. Either the maniac ripped them off or they must have popped while I was hammering him.

The buttons weren't real gold.

But the way I'd lost them, that was golden.

It's past eight, too late to go to practice. I'll go to the war memorial, clean myself up, and head home. My cousin's getting married tomorrow. I hope my hands don't hurt when I raise a glass of wine or have to shake people's hands. And I hope that the police don't come and take me away in handcuffs like they do in the movies. If I killed him, I'll say it was self-defence.

Under the streetlight I check my jeans and my boots. They're covered in blood. Why all the blood? The guy had thin lips, tiny beady eyes, and the yellowy complexion of a lizard. The amount of blood doesn't make any sense. I trudged to the memorial and looked up at the three figures with their machine guns raised. They're a mess too. We've got that in common.

The night is deaf. You can't hear a sound. There's no dawn chorus, nothing of the spring chirping I remember from when I rented a ground floor flat under a thick canopy of trees. Now I'm up on the second floor and the poplars reach my balcony, but there are no birds. Crows and seagulls don't count. They're not birds, they're just part of the urban furniture, skulking around next to the skips until the rubbish truck comes along, hoists the skips up in its iron fist and crushes everything. In the photo I'm holding, our crossbreed is barking, playing in the yard with my aunt's dog. They'd bolted in through the hallway door and were sniffing around under the tables where the wedding guests were seated, already pretty tanked. *Getouttahere*, someone yelled, triggering a game of hunter and hare, one fleeing and the other chasing, both dogs yapping like mad before someone came screaming over from the middle of the room and scared them out into the yard. But it really was a beautiful wedding. A few minutes beforehand, my cousin had tossed her bouquet of flowers over her shoulder, but it got stuck in the plastic chandelier where it had stayed hanging until one of her friends, a real little firecracker, hopped up on the table and made a jump for it. She brought the chandelier down on top of her, tiny shards of plastic lodging in her hair and plunging neckline.

She lay there on her back like a puppy, dying of laughter. When she finally held the bouquet up for everyone to see, the room erupted, and at that moment I put a random record on the gramophone and dropped the needle. Silver Wings. Fucking hell. I immediately lifted the needle, but it was too late. Someone had already started singing *For the Love of a Dark-haired Woman*. The younger guests had again locked arms and were howling at the lone bulb the way lonesome dogs sometimes howl at the moon.

I check the time. It's almost five. A little while now and my mother will wake, sit down with a cup of coffee in the half-light of the kitchen, and wait for me to get up. We've got our plan. She'll take a taxi to the hospital and meet the transfer ambulance coming from Zadar. When they've collected Dad, they'll head south for home. That won't be before ten in the morning, but she'll be up there by eight, supplies for the journey packed and ready to go. By the time they make it to the village, I'll be waiting for them, hopefully with the second concentrator hooked up and pushing oxygen out into what is already a warm spring day.

I'll call Dad's doctor from the road to try to keep tabs on everything. The guy bringing the machine is arriving at noon. It's going to be a long day, but at least we've got time up our sleeve. Everything else is as fragile as my father's life, the one-way traveller, the man taking the motorway south for the last time. That's the only certainty, a bleak guarantee.

We haven't told my brother or my father's sisters that today's the day. We'll tell them when it's all over. Holding back was my idea, and Mum had tacitly agreed. I figured that the fewer people who knew about the trip, the less fear, hopelessness, and grief. And with that being the case, the wide road south would grant us a smoother ride. There'd be no ringing phones. And we wouldn't have to explain anything to anyone.

Words are sometimes as heavy as dark river rock.

Dad, when we were out walking that night, I'm sorry that I didn't tell you what happened. It was the only day or night it ever seemed possible. My fists still hurt, and the epicentre of my distress, which some might call the soul, still ached for some kind of consolation and reassurance. I'm sorry that I couldn't say the words I needed to, as inconsequential as they might have been. Now I've got so much more to be sorry about, so much more that is heavier and darker, and so much still to come. I'm as certain of that as the ticking of the clock. That night, when the four of us stopped to gaze out at the deep, black sea below us, at the handful of stars that appeared in the winter sky as the wind parted the clouds, if only I'd known how to begin. If only I'd found a way to shed the burden, to remove the hump that had germinated on my back.

I felt that face on my fists for days. That breath in my nostrils for months.

*

The trams have started running. We hear them glide by, full of light, the odd bum dreaming his way around another loop in the warm. Mum's turned the light on in the living room, the golden sabre under my door giving her away. Perhaps she's looking for something, or hoping I'll make her a cup of coffee. It's still too early. It's going to be a long, unsettled day and sleep would do us good. But there's no chance of that. I hear her packing, organising her slippers, sorting some clothes into a plastic bag. I'll get up.

'Morning, why aren't you asleep?'

'I got enough sleep.'

'Want a coffee?'

'No thanks, later.'

'Go on,' I try and reassure her, 'go lie down again for a while.'

She goes back to the couch, lies down on her back, and pulls the blanket up to her chin. As I turn the light off, she looks over towards me, the first blue rays of morning light lingering on her face. Dawn had snuck in under the blinds, halted there on my mother's face, and then vanished in the darkness of her eyes.

'You get some sleep too. Don't worry, I'll wake us up on time,' she says.

I returned to my room, somehow calmed by the conversation. I'd left the photo on the pillow, and it was only now that I noticed the creeper on the wall above my father's head. You can't see the shelf, just two light-green tentacles dangling down from the vase, the pathetic colour transporting me back to the living room. That morning they'd taken out the sideboard and sofa bed and brought two more tables and chairs from the neighbour, creating an extension to the kitchen, all the way to the window through which my brother and I, two little scamps, would sometimes climb into our aunt's house. If the dog's barking and carrying on didn't give us away, we'd appear out of nowhere, two happy little ghosts. Hungry. Our aunt would smile and cut us a thick slice of bread. It was either bread and a spread, or else a piece of meat or chocolate. 'Do you want juice?' she'd ask, pointing to a bottle of orange syrup she kept on a doily above the fridge. Of course we want juice.

Having drunk from the same ginormous mug, we'd slip out the backdoor and into the woods where we'd mess about with the other kids. It was in those woods that I once saw a kid have an epileptic fit. I barely knew him. We'd laughed our heads off when the convulsions first started, but we soon shot off and hid behind a tree, yelling for help. When no one came, I ran to the nearest house to find a grownup. But the nearest house was workers' accommodation for unmarried men from the port or the shipyards. The men were all at work, except for one guy who had his leg in plaster. I burst in on him while he was fiddling with something between his thighs. With a few choice words he sent me on my way. By the time I got back to the woods, the boy's parents had taken him home and everyone else was gone. On an oak branch, I spotted a weasel with a bird in its mouth. I sprinted home.

I'd seen death. I was spooked.

The hanging ivy's shiny green leaves stood out against the whiteness of the wall. My aunt had transplanted it from a vase in the hallway, and in just a few short weeks the vine had made it to the floor. It hadn't bothered anyone at the wedding. But it bothers me now, because my father looks like he's surrounded by the kind of wreath you put on a coffin. Those green tentacles were always a bad omen.

And then I remember his voice as he sang that word – *hawk*, a bird which is so perfect in every other way, but never sings. While the contradiction clearly makes a bad song even worse, this morning I feel a certain gratitude for its nonsense. Because with an arm around my uncle, whose eldest daughter was getting married, my father had sung. And the smile never left my uncle's face, even when the young ones started singing for Ustasha officers to come back and save our world, by which they meant Croatia, to come back and battle the enemy led by those two criminals. That would put the world to rights, apparently.

My grandfather had been a Partisan. He was picked up by the Ustasha at the start of the war, but he escaped and was then taken in by the Partisans. He was seriously injured in each of the four years that he fought. When I'd give him a hug, I could feel bits of shrapnel in his neck, bits they hadn't dared extract. They were there on his scalp too, lodged under the skin. My grandfather had borne an MG34, but shrapnel and a lifelong fear of thirst are all he brought home from the war. I hadn't even started school when I first asked him about the Ustasha. Someone in the village had been talking at bocce and had said that the Ustasha were our heroes. Grandad waved his hand dismissively.

'Forget it, boyo, it's a load of bull.'

But I kept asking him, and in the end, he said that they were a pack of bandits.

'And who are the Partisans?' I asked.

'They're slimy creeps.'

We left it at that.

Under my sweetheart's oriel!

I didn't have a clue what they were on about, but my father and my uncle just closed their eyes and repeated this totally baffling word. For a second, I thought that they were singing *under my sweetheart's aerial*, but that didn't make any sense either. Not that the spectacularly stupid original made much more. A hawk is a bird that flies like lightning. It'd have to be a pretty enchanted fairy tale for it to sing under someone's window. That's what I thought at the time. I was an avid reader and carried a neatly-folded interview with Johnny Stulić around in my pocket. *Freedom isn't a divine seed that someone gives you* was the headline. Johnny was standing next to a kiosk, cracking up.

My angel.

*

Mum placed a hand on my shoulder and woke me up. I'd fallen asleep holding the photo, the morning sun having arrived on the night tram, on the face of a tramp, or a drunk, or a security guard from the outskirts, a nightwatchman who keeps vigil over diggers and dump trucks, so no one steals them. I'd met a guy like this once, out front of the bakery next to my building. Bleary-eyed, he sat there on a bench surrounded by sparrows, eating burek and drinking yogurt. I said good morning and sat down beside him to do the same. We shared the sparrows and exchanged a few words.

'How do you steal a digger?' I asked.

'Easy as. Ya load 'er up and drive off.'

'Yeah, but how do you get it on a truck?'

'Haul 'er with a wire rope.'

'Have they ever stolen one on your watch?'

'Nope. But they've stole parts. Chuck 'em through the wire and skedaddle.'

It was a sunny spring morning like that one when my mother woke me with a light tap on my shoulder.

I jumped out of bed, a lightning bolt to the brain telling me I was late. I looked at my mobile and it was just gone seven. Plenty of time. Is Dad awake? Have they got him ready for the trip? It's still early. I want him to sleep a little more.

*

I had a shower and got dressed. My mother was at the kitchen table drinking coffee in her pyjamas. 'Your turn,' I said. We swapped places, and a few minutes later she was back in the kitchen, dressed, hair done, and ready to go.

She didn't want breakfast. We'll have some in the ambulance, she said, trying to sound relaxed. In reality, she'll be perched on a tiny stool at my father's pillow, holding his hand and monitoring the flow of oxygen, occasionally checking the saturation with the gadget she's put on his finger. But she doesn't need that. She just has to look at him to know the percentage, to know how worried she should be.

She can feel the flow of his oxygen in her heart.

'We've got it all organised then. You go up there and collect him, and I'll head south and wait for you at home.'

'I'm scared...' she began.

'Don't be. It's all fine. I've phoned the guy, and I'll phone him again when I'm in the car.'

'And will it actually work?'

'They said it will. Apparently they've set someone else up with a similar system.'

'Apparently?' she shot back. I almost bit my lip.

I need to keep quiet. We both know that the whole operation is precarious, that Dad is terminally ill and in serious pain. We're counting the days and nights we have left with him. That's it.

'Mum, it'll be fine. The most important thing is that we yank him out of hospital.'

Just saying that gave me the yips. Such an ugly word, *yank*, as if he were a tree or a plant, something that could die if uprooted. And again, I had an awful premonition of the horror the day might bring. For him to make it home and see out another month or two, everything has to go exactly to plan. It's the only way to end his suffering in the hospital ward, to free him from the nocturnal binding of his hands and feet, get him out from under the ceiling stains he's condemned to look at until the nurse unties him on her morning rounds. The horror of the image gives me strength, momentarily banishing any doubts. I don't have a choice but to do what he's asked of me. And I should be happy that I can fulfil the simple wish of a sick man, one who seldom expressed any kind of desire of his own, a man always so accommodating, a man who put his own needs second, third, last when it came to his family. A man who never stopped working.

His hands covered in flour, in cement and lime plaster.

I have to block out these images, pull myself together, drive the three hundred kilometres and get everything ready. I'm almost talking out loud to try and reassure myself. But the images return. I see him standing at a long table making braided rolls for Easter, his movements soft and dexterous. I see him tossing plaster up at the ceiling with his trowel, only for it to fall back down on his face and run into his eyes. Next thing I'm holding a rubber hose and he's washing himself in the water. Bloody-eyed, and with his face burning from the lime, he heads off to the night-shift. Behind him, the failure. A job that'll have to wait until he figures out the angle and movement.

Mum heads out to the shop to get a few things. I wait until she comes back so we can go down and wait for her taxi together. As soon as the stinking Dacia appears, our journey will begin. From opposite ends of the city towards a single goal, a house in a village, my father's final wish. A bungalow surrounded by olive trees, a cosy terrace he won't be able reach because of the oxygen tube he'll have to drag behind him like a tail, one that's too short for him to sit out in the sunny spring air. But I'll sort it out. I told the guy with the concentrator to bring a waterproof casing so that we can rig something up for outside.

'Now that it's getting warmer, he'll be able to sit out on the terrace,' I said.

'Certainly is,' the guy replied, 'the cherry trees are already in blossom.'

'Just one final check,' she insisted, combing the apartment, 'make sure I've got everything.'

'No rush,' I replied, already in my jacket, waiting in the hallway in front of the big mirror.

'Is that everything? Got your money for the fare?'

'Course I have. Let's go down and call a taxi from there.'

'Sounds good.'

'But don't forget to call me when you are there. I want a full report. I'll let the doctor know that you'll be up there in about half an hour. Just wait there outside her office, like we agreed.'

'I will. But I'll first stop by and see him for a minute.'

'Have you got a mask?'

'Yes. You know I have.'

Our eyes meet by chance in the mirror. We're huddled together in the narrow hallway, as if before a difficult decision. She quickly looks the other way, opens the door, and hurries to the lift.

I lock up, turning the key twice even though the lock holds fine after a single turn, which is what I usually do. At this point I've become obsessive. I'll lock it twice, so I don't have to think about it. I'll drive slowly, but I won't stop. And I'll keep the ringer on my phone on. When I have to make a call, I'll pull over, but I won't turn the engine off. I normally avoid this kind of hyper-cautiousness, but right now it's all I have to keep me upright and in one piece. Route planning, counting the rotations of a cylinder in a lock, a focus on the trivial, they all help a man face something greater than himself, a summit requiring all his might to scale. He only has one chance, and this is it. On a clear, calm Wednesday in spring, a few degrees above zero. The weather in the village is going to be gorgeous. I checked.

The Dacia soon pulls up in front of our building, the scrawny driver in a mask, his furtive eyes an indeterminate blue. I watch him closely as he opens the opposite rear door for my mother. Everything seems fine. With that same cautiousness, I go over to the driver's side door and tell him the destination through the three-centimetre gap at the top of the window.

'No problem,' he mumbles and takes off. Mum waves. Seeing her go is devastating. I'm all in a jumble, wracked by fear and doubt. My brain's in slow motion. If we're to have a chance, I have to let it all go, shake the feral dog tearing at my leg. But my hands are tied, and now he's on top of me and going for whatever he can.

I went across the road to the shop and bought two cold cans of beer. Then I jammed them in the door compartment, got behind the wheel, and set off. I'll open the first one at the traffic light and finish it by the time I hit the toll booth. When I'm there, I'll open the second, and down it even quicker.

But the cans are going to annoy me, so I'll turn off at the first petrol station and chuck them in a skip from the car window. Then I'll head back out onto the motorway and floor it. With the sun on my temple, I'll drive a hundred and fifty kilometres an hour. Which is exactly how fast my old wheels can go. Having lost reception for Radio Student and knowing that I'm heading into a blackspot, I flick through the stations, feverishly trying to find something else. Charging uphill, I briefly get reception and catch a line from an old classic: *The little man wants to cross the line, he wants to cross the line, but he can't.*

I scream it out with everything I have, almost tearing my vocal cords. When I lose reception completely and even the white noise disappears, I just keep screaming, shaking off the weight and hesitation, flattening the feral dog beneath my wheels, banishing the trembling anxiety. I scream it out, and in doing so, I make my peace with both life and death.

In this mindless hurtling and howling, I didn't hear my phone ringing on the passenger seat, didn't notice it vibrating. Didn't remember that I even had it on me. It was only when I was racing past Karlovac that I glanced over and saw that I had two missed calls. Mum. I froze. Fangs bared, my dog returned. I stopped on the side of the road and called her. She picked up immediately.

'What is it, Mum? Where are you?'

'I'm here outside the hospital.'

'That's great.'

'At Jankomir Hospital.'

'What?'

'The driver took me to the wrong place.'

'What?'

'We told him Jordanovac, but that idiot took off some other way. I told him. I told him that he was going the wrong way.'

'You're kidding. And what'd he do? What'd he do?' I was seething.

'He said that I shouldn't worry about a thing, that we were going this way because of traffic. And now I'm here.'

'Jesus Christ. And where's he?'

'I told him to go. He's probably crazy. Who would know? I don't know anything anymore.'

Then she burst into tears.

I looked at my phone and thought how easy it would be to kill a man, so very easy.

A second later, I snap out of it.

'Listen. Ring another taxi and have him take you to Jordanovac. You'll be late, but we can't help that now.'

'I'll do that, Son.'

'Do you want me to come back?'

'No, of course not. You can't do that.'

'Wait. I'll call you a taxi. Are you right there in front of the hospital?'

'I am,' she sobbed.

I hung up and rang the taxi service. The dispatcher answered quickly.

I explained everything, told him that he had to listen carefully. And listen he did.

'Yes sirree, no problemo.' He sounded like a dick.

In that case, you won't have one either, my inner goon replied.

I decided that when this is all over, I'm going to go to that first taxi company and find that cretin. No hello, I'll just sit him down in his skanky car and tell him what the fucking time is.

'Listen, the taxi'll be there in ten minutes. When you hop in, send me a message and I'll ring you. How's your battery?'

'You know it's fine. We charged them.'

We charged them. We're family, we find a way, we go into battle, and we get Dad out of the hospital. That stirring, heart-warming we, sometimes so terrifying, yet now, a tender almost childlike wonder.

I gunned it out onto the highway. Mum's message arrived soon after, confirming that everything was fine. I called her straightaway and told her to stay on the line until she got out of the taxi in front of Jordanovac Hospital.

'Don't worry, Son, don't worry.'

I pressed the phone up against my ear and in fifth gear drove with one hand for more than half an hour. I could hear the music on the radio in the taxi, but the driver didn't say a word and neither did Mum. I was just relieved that the part of today that had been broken had now been re-glued. When they arrived at the hospital and Mum confirmed that everything was fine, but that she couldn't see an ambulance with Zadar plates, I told her to hurry to the doctor and then call me back.

'I have to go and see him first, first to him,' she said, in near rebuke.

I pulled over at a petrol station. I had enough in the tank, but wanted to stretch my legs at a roadside restaurant famous for its stuffed animals. On their way to the toilet, people pose for selfies with a bear, a fox, a badger, and a rabbit playing belote at a small oak table, all hunched deviously over their cards. The restaurant's got another bear whose back is as high as your shoulder, even though he's on all fours. But he's almost bald, because all the tourists give him a rub when they go and stand in line to order their food. The owner of both the petrol station and the restaurant is a hunter. The whole country seems to know him, but I've only seen him on TV, when he rescued two young bear cubs. He told the cameras: Without their mama, the cubs were orphans, but they're safe now. A super-excited journalist asked him what had happened to their mama. He replied: Poachers probably shot her. That's normally what happens. Then one of the cubs licked him on the forehead, and he reciprocated by kissing it on the snout. The journalist turned to the camera and super-excitedly concluded that this was a story with a happy end. Standing here beside a stuffed bear, waiting for a call from my mother, I couldn't agree more.

But there was radio silence from Mum.

I headed out into the parking area and rang her. When she doesn't pick up, it doesn't take much for me to start sweating sand, to start losing my grip on the slither of hope on which today is built. I only see the darkness. Having risen above the bears, the restaurant, and the hills, my sun has now turned black, but I don't want to see it. I'll call again. No reply.

The doctor is my last hope. It's crossing the line to ring someone who's already been so good to us, who spends her days treating the untreatable, trying to save people's lives and trying to improve their care. But I have to do it. I have to do it before the black nugget of the sun buries me here in this freakish wilderness, alongside four wild corpses playing a bizarre round of cards.

'Hello?'

'I'm sorry to bother you, I'm…'

'Yeah, I know, I know, they've just left, if that's what you were wondering.'

'Yes, that's what I was wondering.'

'I checked the bottle. We got everything organised and good to go.'

'Thank you so much.'

'Let me know how you get on. Send me a text or something.'

'I will. Thanks.'

'Okay.'

'Just one more thing. How was he this morning?'

'In good spirits, in really good spirits,' she replied.

Passing the former animals, I went to the counter, bought a beer, and then headed back to the car, which I'd left running. I drove a hundred metres or so to the far end of the parking area, intending to drink it in peace. Then my phone rang, and Mum more-or-less repeated what the doctor had said. I asked her how Dad had been this morning. She told me that he could barely breathe.

'How was his mood?'

'So-so. He's in a lot of pain. Do you want to talk to him for a second?'

'Yeah.'

I waited for her to take his mask off and then heard an exhausted 'Son?'

And I replied with an upbeat 'Dad!'

Then he asked how it was all going.

I replied that it's all going to plan.

'Good,' he said. 'Let's go home, Son.'

'Here's your mother.'

He gave her back the phone, but she just hung up, probably needing both hands to put his mask on properly, both eyes to monitor his oxygen, and her whole heart to be with him in that moment.

As the ambulance shot south like a bullet.

I almost smashed into the Velebit mountain range, flaming through the tunnel like the spark on a cord of dynamite my parents once lit. Imagining the explosion to come, I burn past the flashing warnings and the speed limits. No reason. No necessity. My boundaries have long been crossed. I've been flipped upside down like a hedgehog on its back, exposed and vulnerable in the places I hurt most. I'm not worried, I can talk anyone around. If the police pull me over, I'll tell them, I'll give them the granular. I've got a photo of a man who can turn blue from oxygen deprivation in under two minutes. I don't care if they're not interested, I'll give them a full report. If it comes to that.

The phone rings as I exit the tunnel. With the light shining in my eyes, I try to stay on the road and answer the call. Braking hard, I let the car almost roll down the mountainside to the sea.

It's the guy with the concentrator. 'I'm at your house,' he says. 'I finished my other jobs a bit earlier than expected.'

I told him that I'd be another half an hour and that he should go run an errand or something. He thanked me and said he'd wait in the car.

'Actually, go wait inside. It's open, and if not, the neighbours have got a key. You can get started. I'll be there soon.'

'Sounds good, mate.'

I went to ask him if he'd brought the extra oxygen tube, so we could extend the line and let Dad go outside onto the terrace. But he hung up, and I floored it.

'Mum, the guy's arrived. He's already there.'

'That's good.'

'How's Dad?'

'He's asleep.'

'Asleep?'

'Yes, don't worry.'

I was soon driving past the village cemetery, then past the priest's house. The whole place was once the primary school where my father was beaten for disobedience. I have clear memories of the cherry trees out the front. Every time we walked by, a whiff of fear and dread would creep up on us, especially in summer when the dark fruit appeared among the deep green leaves. Everything was burnt to the ground in the war. I had mixed feelings about that. Loss, definitely, but also relief, which I could only admit to myself later. It was as if an old debt had been settled, of its own accord. No one cared anymore, but the memory remained. After the war, the diggers arrived and levelled a clearing on which a big villa with an enormous terrace sprung up, the locals surrounding it with kiwifruit vines. Why not grapes? I asked Dad, but he said he didn't know, that kiwifruit were probably in fashion. Kiwifruit are in fashion, yet it was only yesterday that the village kids teased me for eating bananas. What an ape, jungle boogie, that sort of thing. Now they've planted kiwifruit for our padre, the vines providing ample shade for afternoon prayer.

The bell ringer, who was a giant of a man, used to clean the priest's cache of machine guns and hunting rifles in the cool of the back garage. Once he took them all out on the terrace. We watched as he tugged a piece of line with a rag on the end through the barrels, like he was possessed. We kept thinking that at least one of them would go off, that something would happen, but nothing did. So we just stared, transfixed by the precious weapons and their mysterious engravings.

I didn't like the place, so I accelerated, and before long I pulled up in front of our house, my tyres almost skidding.

I parked next to the garden wall and hurried in through the open gate towards the house. I called out, but there was no sound from inside. In the hallway, there was just the one concentrator, plugged in and set out from the wall. Beside it there was a small bag with a transparent rubber tube and a second smaller bag with green plastic fittings. Still sealed in their packaging, two new masks sat on top of the concentrator.

And that was it.

I went numb. Time wasn't on my side. I rang and the guy who was supposed to be waiting for me at home, the guy with the oxygen, quickly picked up.

'I have to fucking go back to Zadar for a new gauge. Someone took it out of the van.'

I didn't understand a thing he was saying. I just collapsed on the couch, steamrolled by exhaustion.

'What now?' I asked.

'I'll be back soon. I can't connect things without that part.'

'How soon?' I barely whispered. I was losing the match. I could feel it.

'Bloody soon. And trust me, some fucking moron's gonna get it.'

'OK, I'll be here.'

I'll call Mum, see where she is. I'll work out the timings, see whether he'll have oxygen when he arrives. Then I gave up because the calculations won't do me any good. How would she know where they are, on which stretch of road. She's in the ambulance, holding Dad's hand and feeding him. Or else just watching over him as he sleeps.

There's no way I could do that. Everything else I can manage, I can cope with. But to see Dad lying there with his eyes closed and a mask on his face, asleep, no. I turn my head away. But the fear twists me back, slaps me, and says watch, watch me as I dance across your brain.

You're mine, all mine.

I opened the fridge and spotted a couple of beers. I took both bottles and went outside on the terrace. I found a pair of pliers on the balustrade and used them to open both bottles, and then took turns drinking from each. I don't know why. The chaos is back. Above me, the corners of the eaves are decorated with swallows' nests. Every year my parents sent about twenty fledglings out into the world. Dad would kill flies with a plastic swat, and then Mum would put them on a piece of paper on an upturned bucket and set it down between the four nests. I remember two chicks falling out and lying there on the ground, unfledged and vulnerable, awaiting a quick death by cat or cold. Mum wrapped them in a rag, climbed up the ladder, and gently placed them back in the nest as two squawking birds circled overhead, the panic-stricken parents of the fallen. She took it all in her stride, just washed her hands and went back to my father, who was in the kitchen. He'd been on oxygen for about a year by then, his movement already restricted. He could cope for about an hour without a mask, which gave him a chance to stretch his legs before he had to go back on the machine for another hour or two. It was a horrible time. We were still adjusting, getting to grips with it all.

Now they seem like days of gold.

The trouble with the swallows wasn't over. Barely half an hour since her last rescue, Mum had gone out into the garden to pick some lettuce, and there, under the same nest, were two more chicks. One was dead, but the other was still moving. At that moment, my uncle pulled up and almost burst into tears when he saw what Mum was holding in her hand.

'Poor little thing, where were you off to so soon? Give me the ladder, I'll put him back.' He was straight into it.

'Don't. They'll push him out again,' Mum protested.

'Which nest did you put him back in?'

'That one up there,' she said, pointing to the closest one.

'He might be from that one over there,' he said, pointing to the opposite corner.

'Well, he could be,' said Mum, deadly serious. Dad was standing in the doorway, holding the oxygen tube.

'Put him back in that nest there and see what happens,' he suggested.

Uncle was up the ladder in a flash.

'Got a cold beer?' he asked Mum.

'I'll get you one.'

Uncle lit a cigarette and put his phone on the table. Then he sat down in a chair, lifted his feet up on another, and took his shoes off.

'I'll keep watch a little, make sure he doesn't fall.'

And that's how he spent the evening. Didn't move, didn't say a thing.

Just smoked and sipped his beer, making sure the chick didn't fall out of the nest.

The nests are empty now. Maybe it's still too early.

How many will there be this year, and will my father be able to see them?

Wee warblers, that's what they called them.

A small white van parked up in front of the house and the driver unloaded a new concentrator, a heavy little unit on castors.

'I'm really sorry. Did I make it in time?' He put the machine down and offered me his hand.

'Yeah, they'll be here shortly,' I said, shaking hands.

He got the unit into the hallway and attached it to a coupling that was already connected to the other concentrator. He then filled a plastic container with distilled water, put it in the slot, and switched both devices on, their motors whirring into life, air hissing from the tube on the floor. He knelt down and held it to his cheek.

'Is it alright?'

'Seems okay, but we'll check it.' He pulled a little gadget from his pocket and attached it to the tube.

'We've got a flow of nine litres,' he said. 'Let's try turning it up.' He set the dial on each machine to eight litres. His little gadget showed a flow of fifteen and a half litres.

'That's that then,' he said, standing up. 'Your mother knows how to adjust it, I brought her the first concentrator too. Just tell her that they always need to be set to the same measure, and from there she can calculate how much oxygen she needs.'

'Just like we just did now,' I said.

'Just like that.'

I offered him a bevanda, but he said no, so I signed his two bits of paper—the rental agreement, and the invoice for consumables and labour. All the calculations above board.

And then I remembered.

'Actually, could you lengthen the tube by a few metres?'

'All done. Everything he needs is in that bag. When he goes outside, just take this tube out and put this longer one in. But don't turn the machines off, it's better to leave them running.'

We said our goodbyes and I found myself alone in the middle of the garden, the two machines whirring away behind me. What a noise.

Lungs are so silent and perfect.

I went to the car to get my bag. I'll stay a few days. I've got nowhere to be. And I'm tired. Ever since I was a kid I've found spring hardgoing. Back then I thought it was the growth spurts and that it was normal to feel so exhausted. I'd sit there holding my thick brown hair in my hands, thinking that the despair brought on by the exhaustion was something fleeting. That it would vanish when I grew up. Sometimes I'd ask my parents what they did in spring when they were children. They'd started working at a young age and didn't remember. Mum would sometimes share something, but my quiet father would just shrug his shoulders.

I was shattered that morning after the wedding when my father had sung. It was around eight a.m., and I was first to wake. I thought someone was knocking at the door, so I leapt out of bed. But there was no one there, just a massive truck loaded with rubbish making its way down the street. A few posts tumbled off the back and rolled across the asphalt. Now that I was up, I quickly got dressed and headed out. The dog was still asleep too, so I called it and we set off back up the hill to my aunt's house. I didn't know what else to do with myself and thought I might have a cup of coffee there. Out here in the morning sun and soft southerly breeze, I wanted to forget the upset from last night, the worry with the young singers and their dismal repertoire. The dog and I practically raced up the hill. There, on the steepest part, a metre-long gash was carved into the grey asphalt. Almost three centimetres deep in places, it was a scar my father and I had left behind. The previous year we'd dug the foundations for the garage, both of us swinging our sledgehammers at an enormous almost impenetrable rock, most of which lay buried in the ground. We would have blown it up, but you weren't allowed to use dynamite anymore. And the rock was right where the garage door was supposed to go.

People on their way home from work kept telling us that we'd never manage. 'You should use a jackhammer,' an old sailor advised us. He drove a white Mercedes, but only on Sundays. On the other days he took the bus to his new job at the shipyards, with everyone else.

'And where'd we get one of those?' my father shot back, almost indignant.

'There's one up top, next to my place. Come up and get it.'

'Whose is it?'

'Belongs to the guys digging the cess pit at Sadik's. C'mon up with me and we'll ask.'

My father dropped his sledgehammer, wiped his hands on his pants, and set off alongside the tall and lumbering man. When Dad got back half an hour later, I was sitting on the rock waiting.

'Go grab the wheelbarrow. We'll chuck the jackhammer in there.'

I sprang to my feet and we almost marched up the hill. The compressor was a big square thing mounted on a trailer. Sadik stood there leaning on the drawbar, which was resting on some blocks. He was our neighbour, and always wore a tie no matter what the occasion. We exchanged greetings and he said that of course we could borrow the compressor and jackhammer, that they belonged to a mate of his.

'You're a lifesaver,' Dad replied.

'But there's no way you fellas are going to manage wheeling it down yourselves. It's bloody heavy, weighs at least a ton. Wait 'til they come back and they'll bring it down with the truck. Hook the fucker up and job done.'

'Nah, we'll just grab it,' Dad replied.

Sadik spread his arms in disbelief. But he didn't say anything else.

First we manhandled the jackhammer into the wheelbarrow together with the thick black tube you connect to the compressor. I wheeled them down to our place, unloaded, and walked back up the hill. Dad was waiting for me next to the compressor, our dog sitting on his foot. That dog adored him.

'We'll take a side each, nice and slow,' he said, grabbing the drawbar and lifting it up off the blocks, angling it slightly.

I grabbed the other side and somehow we got moving, finding our balance as we made our way over about fifty metres of flat ground. We only stopped once, to change sides and give our arms a rest. It was a monster of a thing and the odd neighbour came out onto their balcony or terrace to gawk at us in wonder.

'Little bit more, matey. It'll be easier when we get to the downhill,' said Dad.

'This thing got any brakes?'

'Nup, she's not going anywhere,' Dad replied, wiping the sweat from his brow with his free hand.

We made it to the edge of the downhill part and began a cautious descent. Suddenly, and I knew this was going to happen, the weight of the compressor started shunting us forward, the huge steel box gaining speed on the steep slope. Dad and I tried to hold it back, but we didn't stand a chance. It's over, I thought to myself. I could see us stumbling and the compressor running right over the top of us, before racing onto the road and toppling over, mowing down anyone in its path. And there was always someone out there on that road. I shot a glance at Dad. He was all at sea.

The dog bounced along beside us, barking its head off.

'Let it go!' I yelled, barely managing to stay on my feet. We were still in front of the machine, somehow holding on to the drawbar, the compressor's weight ramming us from behind.

'No!' Dad screamed.

'Let it go!'

Even when walking past today, I can still hear the roar, my deafening command to my own father.

He let go of the drawbar at almost the very moment that I did. The steel nose came crashing down onto the asphalt and somehow got itself jammed, creating the scar. And then everything stood still. In the middle of the road, a little aslant, and with its nose buried in the asphalt, was the compressor. Dad and I, each on our own side, puffing and drenched in sweat.

'Fucking hell,' he whispered. 'Mother of fucking Jesus.'

I didn't say a thing, just sat down on a stone wall overcome with fear. Not because of what had just happened, but because of what this short dramatic episode had brought about. I'd shouted. And in that moment of crisis, my father had listened. I'd got us out of it. I'd saved us.

I'd shouted with such ferocity that today I think the scar in the road wasn't made by a piece of runaway machinery, but by my sovereign, adult voice. My conscious realisation that I exist.

I went over to my father.

'The force of that momentum, all that weight, and then when it starts accelerating...'

'You did well, Son, you did well,' said Dad, patting me on the shoulder. 'Now let's get a fucking truck and get this piece of shit off the road.'

'I'll sort it. I'll go up and see Stevo, the sanitation guy who drives the Tamić.'

I ran up to Stevo's, and we got that piece of shit off the road. And then I took the jackhammer and smashed that blue stone to smithereens. After what had happened, I could have smashed the whole of the Velebit range if I'd wanted. Dad left me to play on my own, which is how he'd put it. He mixed flour. This sort of thing was a world apart.

Everyone at my aunt's house was also still asleep, but the front door was ajar. The tables where we'd been sitting were still there, but the plates, glasses, and tableclothes had been cleared away. The chairs were pushed over to one side. They'd probably danced into the early hours. I opened the fridge and spotted a plate with some prosciutto and cheese. I grabbed a few slices, jammed them in a piece of stale bread I'd found in the pantry, and headed home. The only man awake in the whole wide world, having a sandwich and throwing little bits of prosciutto to the dog. He saves the stale bread for himself, savouring it.

A brand new ambulance stopped outside the front gate. The olive-skinned driver climbed out, followed by a young nurse on the passenger side, both unusually subdued as they walked around to the double-doors at the back. When they opened them, I saw my parents. Mum was sitting at Dad's pillow. He was awake.

'Dad, Dad!' I called out. But not a sound, not even a hand movement, nothing. Mum looked at me, shook her head, and burst into tears.

'Here we are, Pops, we're here, we're home,' said the driver.

He slid Dad's bed out and got it on its castors, the nurse removing his oxygen mask. It's a good twenty metres to the front door. 'Can he make it that far?' I asked. I took his hand and walked beside his bed, the castors rolling quietly on the concrete as Mum and the nurse followed behind us. We stopped outside the door, directly opposite the concentrators, their hum monotonous and relentless.

'The bed won't fit,' the driver said with a worried look.

'It's fine, it's fine, we'll do it this way,' I said.

I went over to the other side of the bed where my father lay, pale, defenceless, and completely oblivious to what was going on around him.

'I'll lift him up, then you drag the bed out of the doorway so I can get in.'

'Okay.'

I got my arms under Dad's knees and armpits, lifting him up as if he were a sick child. Then I carried him inside, laid him down on the sofa bed, and kissed him on the forehead.

Once, twice.

Mum had the oxygen mask back on him immediately.

I headed back out into the yard and thanked the driver and the nurse. They were both very quiet, their compassionate silence terrifying me.

I shook both their hands firmly, as if trying to rouse us all. They left, and I went back inside. Mum had taken a reading of barely seventy percent saturation. Dad had fallen asleep, utterly exhausted. The only thing we could do was to wait and hope that he wakes up.

'You hungry?' I asked Mum.

She hugged me tightly and through a strangled sob said that she wasn't, that she didn't need anything. Just for him to be alright.

'He will be, Mum. We did it, didn't we? He's here, in his own home.'

She didn't reply, just sat down beside him and stared into space.

'You go lie down for a bit too, go on.'

'I will, Son.'

I left them together, closed the living room door, and went into the pantry to rummage around in the freezer. I should've remembered to put out some meat to defrost. It didn't matter. I found a lamb shoulder and dunked it in a bowl of warm water. I'd make soup.

And then I spread flour on the table and kneaded some dough.

Just like my father did for all those years.